First Kiss

"Dance?" Lenny asked.

He wrapped both arms around me, holding me closer than ever before. I was able to relax as we moved to the music. Then he slowed down, until we were barely moving at all.

My head was leaning against his shoulder; my face was turned toward his. He brought his face closer to mine, and I felt his lips brush my forehead in the briefest of kisses. I tried to kiss him back on the cheek, but he turned his face so I was kissing his lips instead, and he was kissing me back.

It was the moment I had been waiting for, and it was even better than I had anticipated. My heart pounded with happiness. I felt like laughing out aloud and shouting to the world. He kissed me!

Books by Linda Lewis

2 YOUNG
2 GO
4 BOYS

WE HATE EVERYTHING BUT BOYS

IS THERE LIFE AFTER BOYS?

WE LOVE ONLY OLDER BOYS

MY HEART BELONGS TO THAT BOY

ALL FOR THE LOVE OF THAT BOY

DEDICATED TO THAT BOY I LOVE

Available from ARCHWAY Paperbacks

WANT TO TRADE TWO BROTHERS FOR A CAT?

Available from MINSTREL Books

My Heart Belongs To That Boy

Linda Lewis

AN ARCHWAY PAPERBACK
Published by POCKET BOOKS

New York   London   Toronto   Sydney   Tokyo   Singapore

AN ARCHWAY PAPERBACK *Original*

An Archway Paperback published by
POCKET BOOKS, a division of Simon & Schuster Inc.
1230 Avenue of the Americas, New York, NY 10020

ISBN: 0-671-60353-6

First Archway Paperback printing February 1989

10 9 8 7 6 5 4 3 2

AN ARCHWAY PAPERBACK and colophon
are registered trademarks of Simon & Schuster Inc.

Printed in the U.S.A.

IL 6+

To my grandmother
and Uncle Al, in loving memory,
and to Aunt Ruth

My Heart Belongs To That Boy

Chapter

One

DANNY KOPLER sat on the park wall looking very satisfied with himself. "You girls are in for the most exciting night of your lives," he announced to Roz and me. "A date to the movies with us boys!"

"Boys? Exactly which boys are you talking about?" I held my breath as I waited for his reply.

His answer was just what I hoped it would be. "Well, to start with, I'm going to take Fran, and Sheldon's going to take you, Roz. And Linda,"—his brown eyes twinkled as he focused on me—"you're going to be asked out by Lenny!"

Roz and I looked at each other and were unable to contain our great joy. We began jumping up and down and squealing, "A date! A date! They're going to take us on a date!"

Not that this was such a big deal for Roz. She had considered herself to be "going" with Sheldon for months now, just as Fran had been "going" with Danny. But *going* meant being a couple together at parties or group events such as trips to the beach or

1

amusement parks. At age fourteen, none of us girls had had an official date.

Least of all me. I had been without a boyfriend for what seemed like ages—ever since this mad crush I had over gorgeous, blond Louie had crumpled when it became clear he had no interest in me. While my best friends, Roz Buttons and Fran Zaro, had gotten closer to the boys they liked, Sheldon and Danny, I just got lonelier and lonelier.

It was not until this week that things began to turn around for me. Due to some matchmaking by good old Sheldon, Lenny and I came to realize that we had special feelings for each other. Then, two nights ago, Lenny had finally admitted to me that the rumors going around the neighborhood were true. He really did like me.

I had gone home feeling wonderful that night. I, Linda Berman, finally had a boyfriend. Someone I could care about and who could care about me. Someone to hold my hand when we walked, to put his arm around me, to kiss me good night, to be with at parties and dances, to always want to be with me and put me first before everything. At least that's the way I always thought it should be when you had a boyfriend, and I was determined to make my relationship with Lenny the best of them all.

Well, so far I had been nothing but disappointed. Except for this one brief kiss Lenny had given me when he told me he liked me, I had nothing to indicate he was my boyfriend. When I saw him yesterday, he acted much as he always did around our crowd— joking around, making wiseguy remarks, getting all the kids to laugh at the outrageous things he said and did.

I laughed too, but inside I was hurting. Why wasn't

Lenny coming over to me, putting his arm around me, treating me as if I were someone special? Had he forgotten that wonderful feeling that passed between us the other night, that highly charged energy that connected just right?

Had he forgotten or had he already changed his mind? Our relationship was so new and I was so insecure in it that I didn't know what to think.

Now Danny's words set my hopes soaring again. If Lenny was going to ask me to the movies, it must mean he really did like me. This date might be the very thing we needed to get things going between us.

"When are they going to ask us, Danny?" I asked breathlessly as soon as Roz and I managed to stop squealing.

"Who knows? Maybe even now." Danny smiled as he looked up the block.

I looked where he was looking and felt my heart speed up immediately. For there in the distance, and approaching at a rapid rate, were the unmistakable forms of Sheldon Emory and Lenny Lipoff.

Sheldon was short and handsome. He had thick black hair that hung down into his hazel eyes and a braces-straightened smile that was simply sensational. While I was the one who discovered Sheldon in the first place, things had never developed between us in a romantic sort of way. Sheldon had wound up going with Roz, and he and I had become good friends. This was all for the best since Sheldon had been the one to help me get something going with Lenny.

Lenny was taller than Sheldon, very thin, and more cute than handsome. His big brown eyes and brown hair that curled around an adorable baby face made him look the picture of innocence. But Lenny was far from innocent. He was the neighborhood clown and the neighborhood mischief-maker. If trouble was to be found, the chances were that Lenny's wise mouth that earned him the nickname "The Lip" was somewhere behind it. Lenny had a scar on his right cheek that he claimed he received in a knife fight. I knew he was kidding about that, but the truth was that Lenny was quite capable of getting someone mad enough to want to stab him.

Lenny had another side to him as well. He could be sweet and sensitive and feeling, with more depth than I had found in any other boy. I don't know what attracted me to Lenny more, his wild and crazy side or his deep and sensitive one. I only knew there was nothing more important to me now than making sure that Lenny really was my boyfriend.

No sooner did he and Sheldon reach the park wall than Lenny began stirring up some trouble. "What's the matter, Kopler, isn't Fran good enough for you anymore? Are you trying to move in on our girls?" he challenged Danny.

"Yeah, Kopler," echoed Sheldon. "Just remember that Roz belongs to me." He put his arm around her as he said that, and she leaned up against him happily. They looked great together, Roz's petite prettiness and long, sand-colored hair and matching eyes contrasting with Sheldon's dark, rugged good looks.

I felt a pang of jealousy as I watched them. If only Lenny would act that way toward me. But Lenny seemed unaware of my wishes. After a brief, "Hi," he hoisted himself up on the park wall next to Danny. He stared at the baseball game that was going on in the ballfield on the other side as if it was the most important event of the summer. If Lenny was about to ask me out on a date, you certainly couldn't tell by his actions.

4

"Look at that fantastic pitch! Unbelievable! He hit it! It's going, going, gone! A home run!" Lenny yelled excitedly.

At his words, Sheldon seemed to forget about Roz. He dropped his arm from her shoulder and sprang to the wall to see what was happening with the game. It was as if Roz had lost all importance.

Roz and I looked at each other in frustration. Why did we have to find boys who were such absolute sports freaks that they would rather watch a dumb old neighborhood ball game than pay attention to us?

Danny, who is on the chubby side and doesn't care much about sports, seemed to understand how we were feeling. He hopped off the wall and put one arm around Roz and the other around me.

"What you girls need is a man that knows how to treat you right," he said teasingly. "Someone to shower you with the attention you deserve; someone who knows how to ask you to the movies!"

The word movies seemed to do it. Sheldon and Lenny turned from the dumb baseball game to glare at Danny.

"Why don't you watch your big mouth, Kopler, before you find my fist stuck in it?" Sheldon threatened.

Danny laughed away his threat. "You think you're so tough, Emory—until it's time to speak up to a girl. Then, all of a sudden you turn chicken, just like Lipoff!"

Lenny's eyes flashed angrily at Dan, then looked up the block. A slow, mischievous grin came over his face. "Well, Kopler, it looks as if you're going to have an opportunity to prove just how great a ladies' man you really are. Since that seems to be Fran coming

5

down the street, why don't you go over and ask her out? Show us how it's done."

Danny's arms dropped from our shoulders. His face turned pale, and then it blushed bright red. It was obvious that, for all his big talk, when it came to asking Fran for an official date, Danny was chicken, too.

This disappointed me. Danny, who had lived in my building until his parents had recently moved away to Queens, was like a big brother to me. He was one of these freaky geniuses who taught himself calculus in the sixth grade and was president of the math team in high school. I always thought of him as more mature than the rest of the boys. Danny knew Fran liked him. What could be so difficult about asking her out for a date?

"Come on, Danny, ask her," I nudged him with my elbow. Something inside of me knew that if Danny blew it now, Sheldon and Lenny would never get up the courage to ask Roz and me. The date to the movies would be over for all of us.

"Fran's crazy about you, you know she is," I reminded him. "She's bound to say yes."

My words seemed to do it. Danny took a deep breath. "Okay, here goes." He walked over to Fran in that slightly waddling way of his.

Watching Danny, it suddenly hit me how tough it must be to be a boy. It was hard enough for us girls to sit around and wait for the guys we liked to ask us out. It would be really awful for a boy to get up the courage to ask a girl for a date only to have her reject him and say no.

Of course, Danny had nothing to worry about with Fran. She positively lit up when she saw him coming her way. She ran her fingers through her frizzy black hair and immediately took off her thick glasses. Her violet eyes glazed over as she blinked up at him nearsightedly. Fran couldn't see a thing without her glasses, but she knew she looked a lot prettier that way. "Hi, Danny. What's up?" she purred in her soft, throaty voice.

Danny must have decided it was best to get right to the point. "What's up is the movies," he announced. "We were talking about a date, just for couples, and I'd like you to come with me. That is, if you—if you want to."

We all waited to hear what Fran would answer.

"Oh, I want to, all right," she said happily. "The question, however, is whether my parents will let me. It might help if they knew what other couples were going." She looked to the wall where Roz and I were standing next to Sheldon and Lenny.

Roz and I looked at each other. Then we looked up at Sheldon and Lenny. Now it was their turn to get red-faced and embarrassed. They squirmed and they nudged each other and they joked and they stammered, but they finally got it out. We girls were all officially asked out on a date for Saturday night. We all had the same answer—yes, if our parents would let us. And we all knew, from dealing with our parents, that was a very big *if*.

My parents are basically okay. They get along with each other, and have good values and all that. But when it comes to me and boys, they're as strict, old-fashioned, and hard to deal with as they come.

Roz and Fran's parents are almost as bad as mine are. Even though we all turned fourteen over the summer, our parents think we're too young to date boys one on one. They don't even like it when we have parties or go to the beach with the boys or hang around in groups on the park wall or by the corner ice cream shop we called the candy store. They seemed to have forgotten what it was like to be young.

This summer had so far been the best summer of my life. Washington Heights, the part of New York City where we lived, was a neighborhood of apartment buildings, mostly six stories high. There were parks, stores, schools, and plenty of kids around. In the summer, most of the kids came out to the park to play ball or just hang around under the shade of the trees. It was a wonderful feeling to be part of the crowd.

This was the first summer that my friends and I had really made it. Not only were we a part of the crowd at the park wall, we each had our own special boy-friend. We wanted to be out with our friends every moment we could.

My parents couldn't understand the importance of it all. They insisted that unless there was a party or special event, I had to have a curfew. It wasn't even a reasonable curfew. Even if the kids were all standing around the candy store, which was on my corner where my parents could check to see what I was doing by merely looking out the window, I had to be home by nine o'clock. It was awful!

I would have been positively humiliated if it wasn't for the fact that Fran had a curfew, too, even if it was a half-hour later than mine. And sometimes Roz did, depending on what kind of mood her father was in. He was the strict one in her house.

Later on the night the boys had asked us to the movies, a whole group of kids had gathered around the wall listening to Lenny tell one of his funny stories. We were having such a great time that nine o'clock came before I realized it. Fortunately, Danny, who has to make all these subway connections to get back to Queens, was aware of the time and came to my rescue.

"Hey, Linda. Isn't it getting close to your bedtime?"

"Bedtime? Huh? What do you mean, Danny?" It took me a while to catch on. Then, with a rush of panic, I grabbed his arm and looked at his watch. It was ten minutes to nine.

"Darn it! Now I've got to go home without hearing the end of Lenny's story," I complained.

"So stay another fifteen minutes," Lenny urged. "What's the big deal?"

"The big deal is that I can't afford to get my parents mad at me tonight. Not if I want them to let me go to the movies."

"Oh," said Lenny. Then his eyes sparkled the way I loved. "Well, since you can't be here for the end of the story, why don't we bring the story to you? What do you say we all walk Linda home, guys? I'm starving anyhow. An ice cream sundae with double whipped cream from the candy store might be exactly what I need."

Everyone was willing to go along with Lenny's suggestion. So that's how I wound up walking home that night in the middle of a whole mob of kids. Lenny was walking next to me, finishing his story, and everyone was laughing.

As we walked down my block, I felt a surge of happiness go through me. It was so great to be fourteen and be part of a crowd and have a boyfriend and my first real date to look forward to. I wished the wonderful feeling could go on forever.

It didn't. In fact, it came to an abrupt halt as we approached my apartment building and I looked up at my third-floor window to see my mother looking out. Apparently, she wasn't quite as happy about my belonging to a crowd as I was. By the expression on her face, you would think I was doing something awful.

"Linda," she called. "It's nine o'clock. Time for you to come up now. Right away!"

I made an attempt to protest. "Aw, Ma, the kids are all going to the candy store for some ice cream. Can't I stay out with them a little longer? We'll be right on the corner, so you don't have to worry."

"No. I want you upstairs now, and that's that," my mother said unreasonably, then turned from the window.

"Come on, Mrs. Berman. Nothing will happen to Linda. We'll be right where you can see us." My friends tried to help me out by calling up to her. They didn't know my parents the way I did. Reason meant nothing once they had made up their minds. Further arguments were only likely to make them angry. And I didn't need to get them angry when I was about to ask for something important like permission to go on a date. It was better for me to just go upstairs quietly without a fight.

"Thanks, guys, but don't waste your energy. My mom's about as flexible as a brick wall," I told my friends. "I guess I'll see you tomorrow."

"See you," everyone called back to me. My eyes sought out Lenny. I was hoping he would walk me upstairs or do something to let me know I was special. But he must have been really hungry because he was already heading to the candy store.

I reminded myself that what really mattered was that he had asked me to the movies. Then I raced up the stairs two at a time to make sure I made it inside before the clock struck nine.

* * *

"Well, I see you somehow managed to get home on time despite your friends." That was my father's sarcastic greeting as he looked up from where he sat at the kitchen table reading a book. My mother was in the kitchen, too, so I figured she must have said something to him about my walking home with all the kids and wanting to stay out later.

Dad and I used to be pretty close when I was younger. Because I loved to read as much as he did, he would always take me to the library with him to pick out books. We both loved nature and would often take long walks to Ft. Tryon Park or down by the Hudson River, or across the George Washington Bridge to New Jersey. Dad wasn't much of a talker, but when he did say something, it was usually worth considering. I knew both Dad and Mom were proud of me because I did well in school and education was the thing that was most important to them. In general, we had a good relationship.

All this started changing when I began to like boys. My parents thought I was too young to have these interests. They were sure liking boys would interfere with my doing well in school. The fact that this hadn't happened didn't mean anything to them. They were always making it difficult for me to do things involving boys and making it clear that they disapproved of whatever I did get to do.

It made for a very tense atmosphere in my house. Like now, as I stood in the doorway to the kitchen, trying to decide what would be the best approach to getting them to let me go on this date.

I picked the "group" approach. I figured my parents would like the idea of safety in numbers.

"A group of us were planning to go see this great

movie together Saturday night," I said cautiously.
"That is—if it's okay with you."

"Group?" My mother looked suspicious right away.
"Just who is going to be a part of this group?"

"Why Roz and Fran, my closest friends." Fortunately, my parents liked Roz and Fran, so I let this
sink in first. "And Danny." My parents loved Danny
because he did so well in school. "And Sheldon and
Lenny, too." I glossed over their names as fast as I
could.

My parents looked at each other. You could tell they
didn't really want me to go. "Are Roz and Fran's
parents letting them go?" my mother asked doubt-
fully.

"Sure they will," I said with more conviction than
I felt. "But that's why it's so important that you let
me go—so we can have a real group, I mean. Roz and
Fran are waiting outside for my answer right now. I
can tell them it's all right with you, can't I?" Plead-
ingly, I gazed from my mother to my father.

My father looked at my mother and shrugged. "It's
up to you, dear." Once he said that I knew I had won.
My mother wasn't about to say no if my father hadn't.

"Well, I guess—if Roz, Fran, and Danny are going
to be there," she began.

I didn't wait to hear anything else. "Thank you,
thank you!" I practically jumped with joy. I raced for
my parents' bedroom where the windows faced the
street so I could let my friends know the good news.

Unfortunately, to reach my parents' room, it was
necessary to pass through the living room. And there,
supposedly watching TV, but obviously managing to
eavesdrop on my conversation with my parents, sat
my brothers, with big, stupid grins on their faces.

Ira and Joey were twins, ten years old, and total

12

pains. They liked nothing better than to tease me about boys and make my life miserable.

As soon as they spotted me, they started right in. "So you're going to the movies with your boyfriend," said Joey.

"We know what you'll be doing there," added Ira.

"Linda and Lenny, hugging and kissing, and all that mushy stuff," Joey said with a silly giggle.

"I don't know how she can stand it." Ira screwed up his face with distaste.

"I don't know how *he* can stand it—yuck, yuck!" Joey held his stomach and made a gesture as if he was going to be sick all over the rug.

Normally, this kind of teasing would require a strong response from me. Even now, I was tempted to go over and knock those twin heads together. But I was able to restrain myself. The last thing I wanted to do was to create a reason for my parents to change their minds about my date.

So I settled for making a face that I hoped was as ugly as my brothers' and for sticking my tongue out at them. Then I ignored those two twin terrors and continued my dash to my parents' room.

I leaned out the window, and saw my friends were still out there by the corner. "Hey, guys!" I called out to them joyfully. "I can go Saturday! My parents actually said I can go!"

"Great, Linda! That's wonderful!" Roz and Fran called back. But I hardly saw them. My eyes were fixed on Lenny as he stood there under the streetlight, smiling up at me.

For a moment, the whole rest of the world seemed to fade away. It was just the two of us, gazing at each other. This strange feeling came over me. It was as if I was connected to Lenny, and I knew that no matter what difficulties lay ahead for us to face, we would somehow always be connected the way we were right now.

"Till Saturday night then, Linda," he said, waving to me and breaking the spell.

I waved back at him and stood by the window watching the kids all head down the block. I couldn't wait for Saturday, and my first real date with Lenny!

Chapter

Two

SATURDAY WAS ONE OF THOSE oppressively overcast summer days. The air was heavy and hard to breathe, and it was constantly threatening to rain. The boys had a softball game going, and when it was over, Sheldon and Lenny sat up on the park wall, talking to Roz and me. We decided to go over to Lenny's house since the weather was so lousy and Lenny was hungry, as usual. I was all excited about this as I had never been to Lenny's house before.

When we got there, his mother was getting ready to leave to visit some relatives in New Jersey. She gave an amused laugh when Lenny introduced her to Roz and me.

"Oh, so you're Lenny's latest little girlfriend." She looked me over. "Aren't you the cutest little thing?"

I guess Mrs. Lipoff might have meant her remarks to be pleasant, but they didn't come off that way. All the emphasis on *latest* and *little* didn't make me feel she thought I was very important or that I was going to be around very long.

I looked at her, but she was smiling a friendly enough smile. I decided to smile back and not worry too much about what she was saying.

She looked sort of like Lenny, with the same smooth complexion, narrow nose, and brown eyes. Her face was young but her hair was completely silver. She wore tons of makeup—dark eyeshadow, false eyelashes, deep red lipstick, and she had long, polished nails. Something about her made me feel uncomfortable, even though she was nice and told us to make ourselves at home while she was gone.

I couldn't believe how different she was from my mother, who didn't wear makeup and would never let me stay in my house alone with boys. In fact, my mother wouldn't even let us do stuff like sit on beds even when she was home.

It didn't seem to bother Mrs. Lipoff one bit that she was leaving us alone in her house. It didn't seem to bother her that the house was a total mess, either.

"Bye, kids. Have a good time and behave yourselves," she said as she breezed out the door. She left a cloud of perfume scent behind her.

"Let's go into my room and listen to some records," Lenny suggested. He led us through a hallway to a room that was even messier than the rest of the house. Clothes were left where they had been carelessly discarded; stacks of newspapers and magazines were piled on the floor; dishes and remnants of unfinished snacks were on the dresser.

Lenny didn't seem bothered by the mess any more than his mother had been. He gestured to the unmade bed. "Have a seat and put on some music. I'll go into the kitchen and see what kind of snacks are around."

Roz and I looked at each other when he had gone. I knew Roz wasn't used to living conditions like this either. Her parents were fanatically clean. The two of us picked up Lenny's bedspread from the floor and tossed it over the crumpled linen. We sat down on the bed while Sheldon chose some records and put them on to play.

I looked around the room and felt sorry for Lenny. The one window faced the wall of an alleyway, allowing very little light to come in. On this rainy day it was almost dark inside, but even on a sunny day I was sure it would be dreary.

It made me grateful for what I had. Although my own apartment had only two bedrooms—one for my parents and one for my brothers—and I had to sleep on a high-riser in the living room, at least the rooms were large and the sun shone in. My mother only worked part time in a neighborhood school, so she was home during vacations and able to cook and clean and keep up the house. And my parents, strict and difficult as they might be, always cared for one another.

I knew this wasn't the case with Lenny's parents. They were separated, and his father had his own apartment. When his parents did see each other, they were constantly fighting. Mrs. Lipoff had to work full time, and when she wasn't working she went out a lot. Lenny was on his own most of the time.

"Sorry there wasn't much food in the kitchen," he apologized when he returned. "But I found this." He held out a bag of potato chips and a bottle of soda.

I tried the potato chips. They were stale, but that didn't stop Lenny. He packed them away as if he was starving, which he always seemed to be.

Sheldon had put on some slow music, and he and Roz got up to dance. I sat on the bed uncomfortably, wondering if Lenny would ask me to dance, too.

He did—after the bag of potato chips was empty. I

stood up and he stood up. Tentatively, he put his arms around me and kind of pushed me around the floor.

It was awkward at first, but after a while I found myself relaxing, my head resting against his shoulder. It was wonderful being there in his arms. His body felt warm and comfortable, and he smelled great, like a mixture of soap and shampoo.

After we danced a few dances, I began to wonder if anything further would happen. Roz and Sheldon had started kissing as they were dancing. Then they sat on Lenny's bed and continued to kiss. I was hoping Lenny would take a hint from them and start kissing me, too.

He didn't. Instead, he stopped dancing abruptly and announced, "I'm developing this awful headache. I'm going to look for some aspirin." Then he left the room.

For a moment, I stood there where he had abandoned me. Then I went over and sat on the bed next to Roz.

"What happened?" Roz asked as she disentangled herself from Sheldon.

"I don't know. We were dancing and it was nice, and I was hoping he'd kiss me. Then, just as I thought he would, he left the room that way."

"You mean he hasn't kissed you yet?" Roz sounded amazed. "Why not?"

"How would I know? Maybe he's shy, or maybe I did something wrong."

"Like what?" Sheldon questioned. I had no answer so he decided to go after Lenny to find out.

"It has nothing to do with you," Sheldon assured me when he came back to the room. "He really does have a headache."

Lenny came in a moment later. "Sorry to be a

party-pooper. This headache just arrived from no-where. Maybe I'm coming down with something.''

I didn't like the way that sounded. "Does that mean you won't be able to come to the movies tonight?''

"Oh, no. I didn't mean that at all. I mean, I'm sure I'll be fine once the aspirins work. I just want to relax now, that's all.''

"Sure,'' I breathed in relief. "I understand. Why don't you lean back against the pillows?''

Lenny did as I suggested. He reached out for my hand, and this gave me some encouragement. He closed his eyes.

I leaned back next to him, holding his hand. This rush of warmth came over me. I wanted to take care of Lenny, to make his pain go away. I had never felt such tenderness before.

I was glad to see that Lenny seemed himself again when it was time for our date to the movies. Roz, Fran, and Dan came up to call for me while Sheldon and Lenny waited in my hallway. When we came down, Lenny started cracking jokes right away about Danny handling three girls at one time.

"You wish you knew how to handle girls like I do,'' Danny answered. He put one arm around Fran and the other around Roz and me.

Somehow we managed to walk across the street that way without banging into each other or stepping on one another's feet. Once we were out of sight of my house, we broke apart into normal couples. Sheldon walked with Roz, and Lenny walked with me. They didn't put their arms around us, however, even though Dan kept his arm around Fran. He was the only one who knew how to treat a girl, I couldn't help thinking.

When we got to the theater, there was an awkward

moment. The boys had asked us to the movies, but they hadn't come out and said they would pay for us. Roz, Fran, and I had discussed this and had decided to come prepared with our own money. We stood back, waiting to see what the boys would do. Fortunately, they did pay for us. That made me feel good. If Lenny was willing to pay for me, it had to be a good sign.

We sat in the back of the theater, off to one side where there weren't many people. Danny went in the row first, followed by Fran, Sheldon, Roz, and me. Lenny was last of all.

"I have to sit by the aisle so I can stretch my legs out," he claimed. Personally, I think he wanted to sit there so he could keep running back to the refreshment stand, buying more junk to eat.

He started off with a large popcorn. He washed that down with a soda. Then he went back for ice cream.

By this time we were well into the movie. I looked down the row and saw Dan had his arm around Fran, and her head was on his shoulder. Roz was cuddled up against Sheldon. Lenny seemed oblivious to this. He was obviously more interested in food than in me.

I tried not to let this bother me. I attempted to stare straight ahead at the movie screen, but my eyes kept drifting to the right and watching the progression of the couples next to me. By now both of them were kissing.

After the ice cream, Lenny decided to take a break from food. He sat there, watching the movie.

I shifted in my seat miserably. Here my friends were kissing away, and I was sitting here doing nothing. I might as well have come to the movies by myself!

Finally, Lenny made a move in my direction. He yawned and stretched out his arms. When he finished, he left his right arm where it had landed—on the back of my seat. He didn't exactly have his arm around me, but it was close.

I sat still, practically afraid to breathe. I didn't want to discourage him, but I didn't want to seem overanxious, either. Very slowly, his hand crept closer to me until it was resting on my shoulder. Shivers went through me at his touch. My attention was fixed on Lenny, as I waited to see what he would do next.

I felt some pressure on my shoulder. Lenny was drawing me closer to him. It was the signal I had been waiting for. I turned to him, put my head down on his shoulder, and threw my arm across his chest. He moved his face right next to mine. I closed my eyes and waited for his kiss.

But then I felt him stiffen. My eyes flew open to see what was wrong. What I saw was Lenny gazing over my shoulder into Roz's curious eyes. Apparently, she had stopped kissing Sheldon so she could watch what was going on with Lenny and me.

What was going on with Lenny and me, from that moment on, was nothing. Once he discovered his romantic actions were being observed by Roz, he gave her nothing more to look at.

"I'm going to get another soda," he announced. He pulled away from me, got up from his seat, and started up the aisle.

"Didn't he kiss you yet?" Roz hardly waited for him to leave before whispering the question to me.

Just my luck, Lenny heard her. He came storming back to his seat. "You better start minding your own business if you know what's good for you, Rosalie Buttons," he warned her. "Or I'll make sure you're good and sorry." He made a fist and stuck it in her face.

21

"Sheldon! Lenny's threatening me!" Roz turned to her boyfriend for assistance. But Sheldon was pointing at Lenny and laughing too hard to be of assistance to anyone.

I looked to see what Sheldon found so funny. It was Lenny's face. In the light reflected from the movie screen, you could see it was all red with fury, and his veins were sticking out on his neck. He was trying his best to look tough, but only succeeded in looking so comical that even I couldn't help laughing. Neither could Danny and Fran.

"Shh! Quiet!" Annoyed voices started whispering from the rows in front of us. We all tried to stifle our laughter. I guess we must have looked pretty funny doing that because Lenny started laughing, too.

When we had all quieted down, Lenny gave Roz a dirty look and sat back down next to me. He put his arm around me, but made no further move to kiss me. At least now I no longer expected him to. Not with Roz sitting there on my other side.

"Sorry for blowing it for you, Linda," Roz apologized to me later when she, Fran, and I went to the ladies' room.

"It's okay, Roz," I told her. "I know you didn't mean anything by it. I guess Lenny's more sensitive than any of us thought."

"Well, you should get another shot at it tomorrow," she said. "Sheldon told me the boys all agreed to go with us to the beach."

"The beach? Lenny didn't say anything about the beach."

"He may not have," said Fran, fluffing her hair in the mirror. "But Roz is right because Danny told me it's all planned."

"And the beach is far more romantic than the mov-

22

ies," said Roz. "I bet Lenny won't be able to resist kissing you once you get him on the blanket in the hot sun."

"I sure hope so," I said. The memory of the way his arms felt around me was wonderful. I couldn't wait to get Lenny on the beach!

To go to the beach with a boyfriend of my own had always been one of my dreams. And now it was actually happening. I could picture myself walking hand in hand with Lenny down the sand, the waves breaking at our feet. He would slip his arm around me, turn to me and kiss my lips, and my heart would soar.

With this wonderful fantasy in mind, I rushed to get ready for the beach on Sunday morning. I stopped only long enough to take a look in my parents' full-length mirror to make sure I looked okay in my bathing suit.

I examined myself critically. The whole picture wasn't bad. Although I was barely five feet tall and not very busty, at least my figure was in proportion, and my bathing suit helped me look curvy in the right places. My thick, shoulder-length light brown hair and eyes that were big and blue made a nice impression.

Unfortunately, when I looked at myself closely, the imperfections were all too obvious. The worst was my nose, which was one size too big for my face. And recently there was my skin, which tortured me by breaking out at all the wrong times.

I sighed. It was tough to be a teenager when looks seemed to be so important. I wished I could make mine to order. I would take Roz's creamy skin and Fran's little upturned nose. But of course Roz and Fran had their imperfections, too, and I wasn't sure I'd want to trade mine for theirs, even if I could.

Anyhow, I had no choice but to accept myself the way I was. I turned from the mirror, threw my shorts and tee shirt over my bathing suit, picked up my bag of beach gear, and ran out to the park wall where we had all arranged to meet.

The ride to the beach was a long one, and I was glad when Lenny sat next to me. He brought with him one of his friends, Billy Upton, and his new girlfriend, Donna Fiori.

"I want you to talk to Donna and make her feel at ease," Lenny whispered to me as we settled in our seats.

This wasn't easy for me to do. Donna was tall, blond, and busty, but despite these assets she seemed to be shy. She hid her height and her chest by stooping as she walked. She clung to Billy for support.

If you asked me, Billy was the wrong one to go to for support. Thin-lipped, hard-faced Billy had a reputation for being mean and a bully. He lived across the street from me, and I knew he was always getting into fights. He did seem a lot mellower around Donna, however. Maybe she was good for him.

By the time we got off the train, Donna had begun to warm up a little. I decided she was basically okay.

"Thanks for being nice to Donna," Lenny said to me as we walked toward the beach. "You're a good kid."

I smiled at him. I was happy to have a boyfriend who cared about other people's feelings. It was one of the things I liked best about Lenny.

Unfortunately, I soon found out something I didn't like about Lenny. The fact that he was supposed to be my boyfriend did nothing to keep him from eyeing other girls. And there, on the beach, was waiting the girl most likely to be eyed—Renee Berkley, the neighborhood flirt.

Renee was with her boyfriend, Louie Fields. That's the same Louie I had once thought I was madly in love with. The fact that Renee was with Louie did nothing to stop her from flirting with anyone else.

The boys all gathered around her as if she was the only girl on the beach. She probably was the only one in a bathing suit like that. It was the skimpiest bikini I'd ever seen. It left almost nothing to the imagination.

Renee seemed perfectly at ease in her near-nakedness. She flitted from boy to boy, watching them squirm.

We girls were squirming too—with rage. "Let's do something to get rid of her," I suggested to Roz, Fran, and Donna.

"Like what?" asked Roz. "None of us can compete with that body."

"Or that suit," said Fran. "Look at Danny. His tongue is hanging out like a hungry animal's."

If we hadn't been so angry, we probably would have laughed at the silly way the boys looked drooling over Renee. Fortunately, we didn't have to worry about her much longer. Louie got tired of sharing her with the other boys. "Let's take a long walk, Renee," he said, clutching her hand and leading her down the beach.

"See you later, guys," she waved as she went wiggling away.

It was only when Renee was out of sight that the boys turned their attention back to the rest of us girls. "How about we all hit the water?" Lenny suggested.

I was tempted to say no just to show Lenny his actions with Renee were not appreciated, but I stopped myself in time. Our relationship was too new and fragile to risk taking that kind of a stand. "Okay, let's go," I agreed.

It was a good thing I did, too, because without Renee's presence, we all had a great time in the water. We jumped the waves, rode them into shore, and bumped into one another. I made sure to be as close to Lenny as possible whenever a big wave came along so we could get tangled up together. It was great!

It didn't take much of this to stimulate Lenny's appetite. After a particularly big wave carried him off to shore, he got up and announced, "I'm starving! Anyone for the boardwalk and some food?"

"I'll go," I said eagerly, hoping to have a chance alone with him.

No such luck. Everyone else decided to come along to the boardwalk. Lenny polished off two hamburgers, a hot dog, french fires, a large soda, and an ice cream. I guess the food put him in a good mood because he then suggested going to the amusement area of the boardwalk so he could win a prize for me.

Some of the other kids tried their luck at the games but soon gave up. Not Lenny. He kept putting down more money and playing the games. Everyone gathered around him to watch and cheer him on. When he scored he whooped it up and the crowd hollered and clapped. When he missed he banged the game board and let out this awful sigh. He really got into what he was doing.

Fortunately, he was good at it as well. It took him a while, but he won this giant panda bear for me. I was bursting with pride as I carried it back to the beach.

Louie and Renee were back on the blanket by the time we got there. Renee took one look at my bear and decided she had to have one, too. "Ooh, Louie! Win me a bear. Pleeease, Louie."

"All right, Renee," Louie sighed as he went to his pants to get his money. He didn't know how to say no to Renee.

"You're such a sweetheart, Louie," Renee wrapped her arms around him and led him toward the boardwalk. It was disgusting.

"That Renee. She can't stand the fact that someone else might have something she doesn't have," commented Roz.

"Well, she's going to be getting exactly what she deserves tomorrow," noted Donna.

"What's that?" Fran asked eagerly.

"Take a look," Donna pointed to where Renee was walking off into the distance. From the angle where we stood you could clearly see that some of the skin that was revealed by her bikini had never been exposed to the sun before. While the rest of her body was a nice, deep tan, the cheeks of her backside were already turning a brilliant, sun-burnt red.

"Wow!" said Roz. "I bet she's going to be so sore she won't be able to sit down."

"We'll really miss her at the park wall," Donna said sarcastically.

We girls all laughed together. As we did, I realized that even though she was tall and we were short, she was busty and we weren't, Donna Fiori was already one of us.

Today had been a great day. I'd acquired a new panda bear and a new friend, too. Now if I could get Lenny to kiss me, everything would be perfect!

Chapter

Three

EACH NIGHT AFTER THAT, I fell asleep with my panda bear in my arms. I thought of Lenny and wondered if he was thinking of me. Each day I woke up hopeful that this would be the day our relationship would make some progress. That this would be the day he would finally kiss me.

But each day came and went with no further development. All the kids went about their business, going to summer school or summer jobs, then out to the park wall to see what was going on. Lenny had a job delivering groceries for a local store, but since it was only part time he was around pretty often. The only work I had been able to get was occasional babysitting, so I was usually around, too.

Unfortunately, so were most of the other kids at one time or another. Lenny and I had no opportunities to be by ourselves. And I had learned from the experience with Roz that Lenny was not about to make any move toward me if there was anyone else around to observe it.

I tried to think of ways to be alone with Lenny, but I didn't know how to do it without seeming obvious. Then one hot afternoon, as if he were reading my mind, Lenny mentioned how thirsty he was for this frosty pitcher of grape juice that was sitting in his refrigerator. He asked me to walk him home to get some.

It was the opportunity I had been waiting for. "Sure, I'll walk you," I said, as if it were no big deal.

It was. I found my heart pounding with fear as we approached his building. For one thing, I knew my parents would have a fit if they found out I was alone with Lenny in his apartment. For another, I was afraid of what might happen if something went wrong.

What if I was alone with him and he still didn't kiss me? Even worse, what if he did and decided he didn't like the way I kissed?

As he turned his key in the lock, I almost chickened out and told him I would wait outside while he got his drink. But something told me it was now or never. Lenny had been my boyfriend for almost two whole weeks. If our relationship was ever going to go anywhere, I would have to take the chance.

We went into the kitchen, where Lenny found the pitcher of juice and two glasses that looked fairly clean. The table was too messy to sit at so he suggested we go into his room.

Even though the day was bright and sunny, Lenny's room was almost as dark as the last time I had been there. This time, he did make a slight effort to straighten it. He smoothed out his sheets, picked up the crumpled spread from the floor, and tossed it over his bed.

"Have a seat," he said, sitting down himself. He leaned back against the pillows and drank his juice.

I hesitated. I could hear my mother's voice in my head saying, "No sitting on beds, Linda." I shut the voice out and sat down next to him. I busied myself studying the grape juice. Beads of water were condensing on the glass and running down the sides.

Lenny finished his juice. "Want to hear some music?"

"Okay." I breathed a sigh of relief. Listening to music meant I didn't have to think up something to say to him.

Lenny got up and looked through his records. I sipped my juice very slowly. He sat next to me, seemingly engrossed in the music.

I could only make the juice last so long. When it was finished I put my glass down on the dresser. I sat perched awkwardly on the edge of the bed.

"Dance?" Lenny asked.

I stood up, grateful to have something to do.

He wrapped both arms around me, holding me closer than he had ever done before. I was able to relax as we moved to the music, and, as we moved, he began to slow down until we were barely moving at all.

My head was leaning against his shoulder; my face was turned toward his. He brought his face closer to mine, and I felt his lips brush my forehead in the briefest of kisses. I responded by trying to kiss him back on the cheek.

As I did that, he turned his face so his cheek was no longer there. Instead, I was kissing his lips, and he was kissing me back.

It was the moment I was waiting for, and it was even better than I had anticipated. My heart pounded with happiness. I felt like laughing out loud and shouting to the world. He kissed me! Lenny finally kissed me! He really is my boyfriend now!

By the time we left Lenny's apartment and returned to the park wall, both of us were very accomplished at kissing. It was like nothing I had ever experienced playing kissing games at parties. It was nothing like the brief kiss Lenny had given me when he first told me he liked me. Lenny and I had shared something special and wonderful, and it showed all over us.

Roz didn't have to ask if Lenny had kissed me now. She took one look at us and laughed. "It looks like you two had a productive afternoon."

"I told you before to mind your own business, Roz," Lenny warned. But you could tell that this time he wasn't really angry.

"Well, if you really want me to mind my own business, I guess I shouldn't tell you this important piece of news. But since Linda is my friend, I'm going to say something anyway. Your mother came by the wall about a half hour ago, Linda. When she saw that you and Lenny weren't here, she began asking all sorts of questions about where you could be."

"She did?" I gasped. "What did you tell her?"

"That you had been here with us until you took a walk with Lenny. But I made it sound as if you had just left."

"You did? Thanks, Roz. But now I've got to think of something to tell my mother about where I've been."

"Why don't you say we took a walk to Ft. Tryon Park?" Lenny suggested. "Tell her we wanted to look at the scenery."

"Ft. Tryon? That's a great idea, Lenny." I looked at my watch. "If I really run, I have just about enough time to make it up there and back before supper."

"Wait a minute. You mean you want to go all the way up to Ft. Tryon now?" Lenny asked. "Why?"

"So when I tell my mother I went there I won't be lying. Want to come with me?"

"Are you kidding? Ft. Tryon must be a mile each way. Besides, going there won't change the fact of where you spent this afternoon, anyhow."

"I know," I sighed. "But it's the only way I can handle this. Believe me."

"Okay," Lenny shrugged. "Do it your way if it makes you feel better. But what's going to make me feel better is to sit right here up on the wall. I'm tired!"

I was tired, too, but it didn't matter. I had to go up to Ft. Tryon and back. I hated to lie. Actually going to the park was the only way I could deal with the guilt I felt for having disobeyed my parents by going to Lenny's house.

Even though my parents accepted my story about going to Ft. Tryon, they were still angry enough to punish me. "What were you doing alone with that boy in the park, anyhow?" my mother demanded. "Look at yourself! Your clothes are all wrinkled and disheveled. Nice girls don't act like that!"

"And nice girls don't pick boys like that for boy-friends," my father added. "He's not the kind of boy we want you to have anything to do with."

"Why? What's wrong with Lenny?" I asked defensively.

"Lots of things," my mother answered. "When I found out you went off with him this afternoon, I called Mrs. Kopler to see what she knew about him from his association with Danny. She had nothing but bad things to say about that boy. He comes from a

32

broken home, cuts school, and has a fresh mouth. Keeping Danny away from boys like that one was the main reason the Koplers moved from this neighborhood out to Queens.''

"Well, that shows how ridiculous they are!" I said hotly. "Danny comes here almost every day by subway to see his friends. There's nothing wrong with them, and there's nothing wrong with Lenny. He can't help coming from a broken home. If he cuts school once in a while he's smart enough to make up for it. As for his mouth, he's just got a lot of personality and spirit. Mrs. Kopler doesn't know how to appreciate him, that's all.''

"Well, we don't appreciate him, either," said my father. "Especially when he takes you off to parks alone. That kind of thing leads to trouble!"

"I'm not going to get into any kind of trouble," I protested. "I'm not a baby anymore. Have some faith in me!"

"It's not you we don't have faith in," my mother said. "It's that boy. He's a smooth talker—Mrs. Kopler warned me of that—and you're young enough to fall for his lines and his charm. If you know what's best for you, you'll keep away from him!"

Then came the punishment. "You're not to go out after dinner tonight, Linda. You need some time to think over what we said to you."

I did think things over, but not with the results my parents wanted. I thought about what it was like this afternoon with Lenny, kissing him. I thought about the way his lips felt touching mine, the warm closeness of his arms.

There was nothing bad about what we had done—nothing. My parents were so fearful about everything themselves that all they wanted to do was transfer that fear to me. Well, I wasn't going to accept that fear. It was bad enough that I had to accept rules that didn't make sense and punishments over nothing!

"We're going outside, Linda. Too bad you have to stay in!" My brothers' taunting words broke into my thoughts. I was already so miserable that nothing they could have said would have made any difference. All my friends would be out now, having a good time while I was stuck here in the house.

I had worked myself up to an extreme state of self-pity when I heard this sharp, familiar whistling sound in the street. Hopefully, I raced to the front window. There was Lenny, standing in the street and looking up at me.

"What happened to you?" he asked.

"My parents are making me stay in tonight to think things over."

"Oh. Well, even prisoners are entitled to basic privileges. Think they'll let me come up and visit?"

"Better not. It'll only make them angrier," I said unhappily.

But just by standing there and talking to me through the window, Lenny managed to cheer me up. I was actually starting to feel good when my parents called me to get inside.

"So that boy couldn't be without you for one evening," my mother commented nastily.

"His name is Lenny, not 'that boy'," I told her.

My good feelings vanished. All Lenny had done was to try to cheer me up. Why did my parents resent that? It was as if all they wanted was to see me miserable!

My relationship with my parents was deteriorating rapidly. They refused to accept that Lenny was my boyfriend. They seemed to go out of their way to create problems for me—to watch my every movement, to criticize whatever I was doing, to find excuses to punish me constantly.

One day my mother was looking out the window and saw Lenny kiss me on the street. She absolutely flipped out. As soon as my father came home she started working him up about what had happened. He came after me at the park and dragged me home as if I was a little child. Not only that, he threatened Lenny that if he ever came near me again he'd be good and sorry. All the kids witnessed this. I was positively humiliated to be treated that way in front of my friends.

I tried to make my parents see that I hadn't done anything so terrible. At my age, it was natural for me to want a boyfriend; the hugging and kissing were natural, too. To me, being in Lenny's arms was the warmest, cuddliest, most terrific feeling in the world. There was nothing wrong with it, but my parents didn't understand.

They were totally close-minded when it came to Lenny. They had decided they didn't like him based on what they had heard about him, and that was it. They never got to know Lenny well enough to see how much good he had in him.

Of course, even I had to admit that Lenny often made it hard to get to know him. He covered up his deep feelings and sensitivity with his wise-guy, bigmouth attitude. Most people never got to really know him.

Since we had started going together, I was seeing more and more of the good side of Lenny. I found we could talk to each other about anything.

He told me about how awful it was to grow up in a

home where his parents were always screaming and fighting. He told me about the turmoil he almost always felt inside. He talked to me about school, which he had done well in when he was younger, but he was now finding it increasingly difficult to sit and listen to what the teacher was saying.

One night, Lenny seemed especially tense when he arrived at the park wall. He asked me to take a walk with him, and we went to sit on the terrace in back of the park. From there we could watch the sun set over the Hudson River and the George Washington Bridge.

For a while we sat without talking, watching the colors changing in the twilight sky. A soft breeze blew up from the river. Even without touching Lenny, I felt very close to him. I sensed he needed this time of quiet. Patiently, I waited for whatever it was he had to say.

"My father came home tonight," he finally told me. "He hardly ever does that since he took his own apartment, but he had something he wanted to discuss with my mother.

"Oh." I didn't know what to say to that. "Well, how did it go?"

"Terrible." He took a deep breath. "My father can be a really nice guy when my mother's not around. But put the two of them together and they both become screaming lunatics in no time. I can't stand being in the house with them. It got so bad I finally left without eating any supper. I bet they didn't even notice I was gone. They were too involved with destroying one another."

"Oh, Lenny. How awful. Was it always like that with them?"

"Ever since I can remember. In fact, it got so bad sometimes they would pull knives on each other.

36

When I was little, it would scare me so badly I would run into my room, hide in a closet, and cry. I was sure they would kill one another. Now I realize the chances are they won't. But it's horrible to be with them just the same."

"I bet it is. My parents never scream and fight with one another."

"Never?"

"Not that I can remember. Oh, sometimes they have disagreements and heated discussions, but they don't fight—at least not in front of my brothers and me. But then again, they don't show much positive affection in front of us either. We almost never see them hug or kiss or say they love one another out loud. They don't hug or kiss us or tell us they love us much either."

"That's interesting. My mother likes to hug me and she tells me she loves me all the time. Of course, in the very next breath she can tell me she hates me. Very emotional. While it sounds as if your parents don't show much of any kind of emotion."

"I guess they don't. But don't get me wrong, Lenny. It's not that my parents don't love each other or love my brothers and me—they do. They're just kind of reserved about it."

"Well, at least you're not reserved about showing affection—not to me, anyhow!" He put his arm around me and hugged me to him.

"No," I breathed, as I hugged him back happily. In fact, one of the things I liked most about my relationship with Lenny was that we were both comfortable showing affection to one another. I needed that feeling of having him hold me in his arms.

We talked more that evening about how our parents affect us without our even knowing it sometimes. Lenny admitted he had been afraid of getting into a relationship because of what he had seen with his parents at home. He told me he was glad I wasn't anything like his mother. She got him upset while I was able to calm him down.

I felt so close to Lenny that night, I thought nothing could go wrong with us. Then Ellen Rossi came back into our lives.

Chapter

Four

DURING THE WINTER, around the time I had my crush on Louie, Lenny and Ellen Rossi had been going together. Ellen was too heavy, but she had a few assets like a pretty face and a big bust. Ellen never worried about stuff like if it was proper to chase after boys. She was a born flirt and would do things like plop herself down on a boy's lap and run her fingers through his hair.

Ellen and Lenny went together on and off for months. They had a stormy relationship with lots of fights, breakups, and make-ups. Then Ellen had started going out with Nicky James, this tall, gawky, freckle-faced boy, who at one time had had a crush on me. Ellen and Nicky had broken up right before Ellen had gone away to summer camp.

I was very glad that Ellen was away while I was first going with Lenny. I wanted our relationship to have a good foundation before she came back. I always knew that if Ellen was around, it could mean trouble for Lenny and me.

But summer couldn't last forever. And on the first cool day that hinted of fall, the word spread throughout the neighborhood that Ellen had returned.

The next morning was Saturday. I was on my way with my mother to go shopping to buy some things for the new school year, when I ran into Fran. She was the one who broke the news to me.

"I'm going over to Ellen's," she told me. "Danny's supposed to meet me there later, along with some of the other kids. I think Lenny will be coming, too."

"Lenny?" I felt this clutching in my stomach. "He didn't say anything to me about going to Ellen's."

"No?" Fran shrugged her shoulders. "Well, maybe I'm wrong. Try to come by anyway."

Now my entire morning was ruined. I knew Fran didn't make that up about Lenny's going to Ellen's. She must have heard it from Dan who probably heard it from Lenny. But Lenny hadn't said a word to me about going to Ellen's. That meant he didn't want me to know, which meant he had motives for going that I wouldn't be very happy about.

All through the shopping trip I kept thinking of Lenny and Ellen. What if she had lost weight during the summer and looked positively gorgeous? What if he decided he still liked her more than he liked me? By the time I arrived back home I was burning with anxiety. What had happened while I was gone?

I decided against going to Ellen's. Instead, I would sit up on the park wall and wait for someone to come along who knew what had been going on there this morning. Once I had the picture, then I would decide what to do.

Danny and Fran were the first ones to appear. They had good news and bad news. The good news was when Fran had told Lenny I knew he was up there at

Ellen's, he said he had no intention of going after her. The bad news was that he, along with Nicky, Sheldon, and Roz, was still up at her house.

After a while, Sheldon and Roz came along. "Boy, that Ellen really changed over the summer," Roz reported. "She seems quieter, more mature—almost sophisticated. I think she's lost weight, too."

"Oh, really?" I pretended to be indifferent. This was not what I needed to hear. I began working myself into a terrible state of mind. Lenny knew I would be back early from shopping. Why would he still be up at Ellen's house unless he was interested in her again?

I could picture Ellen right now, sitting in Lenny's lap, her chubby arms thrown around his neck. I could hear her telling him how much she missed him and bringing her lips so close to his that he couldn't resist kissing her. I started feeling as sick as if this had really happened.

That's when Lenny showed up, walking toward the wall, accompanied by Nicky. I saw him coming and didn't know how to handle it.

What do you say to your boyfriend when you know he's just come from his ex-girlfriend's house? Do you ask him if he enjoyed himself, if he still found her attractive, if any old feelings are still there? Do you pretend that you're so secure you're not worrying about it one bit? Or do you get angry and tell him he had some nerve visiting her when he's supposed to be going with you?

I didn't know what was the right way to act with Lenny. I certainly didn't know what was the right thing to say. Out of fear of making the wrong decision, I wound up not saying anything to him at all.

"Hi, Nicky," I said, totally ignoring Lenny. "Did you have a good morning?"

"Oh yeah." Nicky looked at Lenny and laughed. "We had a great morning, didn't we, Lenny?"

"It was okay." Lenny sounded annoyed as he said it. I was hoping he would say something to explain the situation and make me feel better, but he didn't. He spotted Billy coming down the street and walked over to talk to him. He spent the rest of the afternoon talking to Billy, Sheldon, and Nicky. It was as if I wasn't even there.

Now I felt really awful. I knew I shouldn't have ignored Lenny when he came to the wall. He probably figured I was mad at him, and of course, I really didn't have any reason to be mad at him—except for what I was imagining in my mind.

But it was too late to do anything about it now. There was nothing I could think of to say or do without making myself look like a fool. So I hung around the wall, talking to Roz and Fran and feeling miserable.

That night, Danny stayed over at my house. My mother and his had arranged it so he wouldn't have to go back home on the subways late at night when it was so dangerous. My mother put up a cot for him in my brothers' room.

I was hoping that with Danny around, we could get another couples' date going. Lenny and I would have a wonderful time, and he would tell me I was the only one for him. It didn't work out that way. Roz was being punished by her father for some little thing that she had done and wasn't allowed out that night. Donna was stuck home baby-sitting for her two little brothers. Instead of making an effort to get things right with me, Lenny went off with Sheldon, Nicky, and Billy to organize a card game with some other boys in the neighborhood.

There was nothing for me to do but to go over to Fran's with Danny. I felt like I was in the way there, hanging around with the two of them. To make matters worse, Ellen called to speak to Fran. I had to drag it out of her, but Fran finally admitted what Ellen had told her.

"Ellen says she had forgotten how cute Lenny was over the summer. She would find it very easy to start liking him again."

"Oh, she would, would she?" I said angrily. "Doesn't she know that Lenny is now *my* boyfriend?"

"See, there you go getting all hotheaded, Linda," said Fran. "That's why I didn't want to tell you what Ellen said. Besides, it doesn't make any difference whether Ellen likes Lenny. What matters is who Lenny likes—Ellen or you!"

"What's wrong with his liking both?" Danny put his arms around Fran and me and hugged us together. Fran squirmed loose from him and hit him over the head with a pillow for that remark. But to me, it was serious.

"Maybe Ellen's willing to go along with a situation like that," I said. "But I'm not. Lenny's going to have to make up his mind which one of us he wants!"

"Why don't you take it a little easier, Linda?" Danny suggested. "Things have a way of working out. If it's meant to be for you and Lenny to stay together, something will happen to get Ellen out of the picture. If it isn't—well, you're better off finding out Lenny's not for you before you get too serious and really get hurt."

"It's too late for that already," I said glumly.

Dan and Fran laughed, but I wasn't kidding. Lenny and I had only been going together a little over a month—not a very long time, to be sure. But time had nothing to do with the way I felt about Lenny. He had to choose me over Ellen. He had to!

I was very nervous, not knowing what to expect the next morning when our crowd met at the park wall to go to the beach. Fortunately, Ellen wasn't there, and Lenny was in a good mood because he had won at the card game. When we got to the beach, he organized a "chicken fight." The girls climbed on the boys' shoulders, and everyone tried to knock each other into the water. We were all laughing so hard that any hard feelings seemed to be forgotten.

But a little later, when we were up on the blankets drying off, things abruptly changed. "Uh-oh. Look who's coming," Donna announced.

I looked up and my heart sank. Renee Berkley was making her way toward us, but it wasn't Louie who was accompanying her today. It was the person I least wanted to show up on the beach, Ellen Rossi. And she had lost enough weight over the summer to risk being seen in a bikini almost as skimpy as Renee's.

If you asked me, she was still too fat for a bikini, but nobody bothered asking me. I saw Lenny eyeing her appreciatively as he pretended to be busy digging a hole in the sand.

I was tempted to go over and step on his head, but I controlled myself. Instead, I made a supreme effort to be big and went over to greet Ellen.

"Hi, Ellen. How've you been? Did you have a good summer?"

"Sure did. Camp was great, even though the food was awful. But then again, that's how I lost the weight to fit into this bikini!" She giggled and twirled to show off her new figure.

The boys all responded to this with whistles and

howls. Ellen absolutely ate it up. "Anyhow, I'm glad to be back. I hear you and I have something in common now, Linda."

"We do? What's that?"

"Lenny! We've both gone out with him now."

"Oh yeah, Lenny." I tried to smile, but I couldn't. I knew what she meant by this statement. We both went out with Lenny so that made us equals. She regarded Lenny as fair game.

Well, I didn't look at it that way. Lenny was my boyfriend now. Ellen had had her shot at him, and she blew it. She wasn't going to come between us if I had anything to say about it.

But as I was thinking of something clever to say to let her know all this, Ellen lost interest in talking to me. She walked to where Lenny was digging and began to fuss over him.

"Oh, Lenny! Look at that hole you're making! It's got to be the biggest hole I've ever seen! Soon you'll get down so deep you'll hit water!"

What a jerk she looked, making a fuss over a stupid hole. But Lenny didn't seem to realize Ellen was being a jerk. He was too busy staring up at the view of her bikini from the perspective of his hole.

"I've hit water already," he said, hoisting himself onto the sand. "Time to give up on this hole."

"Good!" Ellen giggled. "Because this ocean air has given me an appetite. Why don't we go up on the boardwalk and see what there is to eat?"

All anyone had to do was mention food to Lenny and he was already salivating. "Great idea—I'm starved," he agreed. Then, as if an afterthought, he added, "Anyone else for the boardwalk?"

Once Lenny said that, all the other kids decided to come along. All except me. I wasn't about to chase after Lenny as he did exactly what Ellen asked him to.

Instead, I sat on the blanket by myself and took out the lunch I had brought from home. It was a peanut butter sandwich. I took a bite out of it and chewed. Yuck! Somehow it had gotten full of sand. Disgusted, I threw the sandwich away. I wasn't really hungry, anyway.

I lay back and watched the clouds drift across the sky. Was I doing the right thing by not following Lenny to the boardwalk? Did I come off as cool and above it all, or was I being a fool and playing right into Ellen's hands?

I rolled over onto my stomach. It seemed a long time that everyone was gone. Maybe I should go to the boardwalk and see what was happening. But then I would look twice as silly, as if I didn't trust Lenny with Ellen. After all, there were lots of other kids there with them. What could be going on?

I found out a short time later, when Roz and Donna returned from the boardwalk. They brought with them nothing but bad news.

"Some of the kids are playing the games again," Roz reported. "Would you believe that dumb Nicky is wasting his money trying to win a teddy bear for Renee, even though he knows she's Louie's girl and has no interest in him?"

"If you ask me, Lenny is even dumber," said Donna. Then she looked at me and clapped her hand over her mouth. "Sorry, Linda. I shouldn't have said anything."

"Don't be sorry. Tell me what you were about to say," I urged, even though something told me I wasn't going to like it.

I didn't. "Lenny's trying to win a bear for Ellen," Donna admitted.

"Not that he wanted to—she just kept begging him, so he couldn't refuse," Roz tried to explain.

"Sure he could have—if he cared anything about my feelings," I said sadly. "How quickly he forgets that I'm the one who's supposed to be his girlfriend."

It was bad enough to think about Lenny there on the boardwalk with Ellen. But when, a few minutes later, I saw them actually walking back to the blanket together, a little bear displayed proudly in Ellen's arms, it was more than I could take.

Leave it to Ellen to rub it into me. "How do you like my new teddy bear, Linda? Isn't it cute? Wasn't it sweet of Lenny to win it for me?"

I was filled with this urge to tear that bear from her chubby fingers, throw it in the hole Lenny had dug, and bury it so deeply it could never be found again. I fought it back. The last thing I needed to do was show how jealous I was in front of all the kids. But I knew that if I stayed in that situation, I wouldn't be able to control myself much longer.

"Real sweet!" I managed to force out the words. Then I whirled around and stalked off toward the ocean and began walking along the water's edge. I had to be by myself just then. I had to walk off the tension. I had to let the wind that whipped off the water and the waves that lapped against my feet carry away my anger, hurt, and pain.

I knew Lenny would probably be annoyed at me for running away—it wasn't the way he liked me to act.

But what did it matter? If he really cared about me and having me for his girlfriend, how could he have treated me this way? How could he be so uncaring

47

about my feelings as to openly choose Ellen in front of everyone?

I was hoping Lenny would at least try to talk to me on the way home from the beach, but he didn't. And I didn't trust myself to attempt to talk to him. I was too afraid I might lose my temper or say something to make the situation worse.

All the next day while I was baby-sitting, I thought of Lenny constantly. Although we had only been going together a short time, he was already a big part of my life. We had shared so many thoughts and feelings and wonderful times. Why did Ellen have to come along to ruin everything?

That night, our crowd was hanging around the candy store by my corner. I looked out my window and saw that Ellen wasn't there, but Lenny was. I went downstairs, hoping this might be the time to set things right between us again.

Lenny was standing in the center of the group when I got there. He was telling a joke, and he had everyone laughing at how funny he looked and talked. He was laughing, too, obviously enjoying the attention he was getting.

I felt like an outsider among my own friends. I tried to join in the laughter, but I wasn't really part of it. How could I be when inside I was numb with fear about what might happen to Lenny and me?

For a while I managed to put up a front, joking around with some of the other boys. I wanted to show Lenny that I could have a good time no matter what was going on with him. I wanted to believe that if I ignored the tension between us, maybe it would go away.

It didn't. I noticed Lenny kept checking his watch.

Finally he said something to me. "Linda, I'd like to talk to you. Why don't we go sit in your hall?"

"Okay," I said numbly. I followed him into my building. We sat on the steps between the second- and third-floor landings. It was a spot we had often come to before, to be alone and talk together, a spot we had stood at, kissing each other good-night.

It had always felt good to be with Lenny at that spot—until now. I leaned against the wall for support and stared at him through frightened eyes. I waited for what I knew was coming.

"Linda," he began. "It's hard for me to say this to you, so I want you to just try to listen."

I sucked in my breath. After this kind of beginning, what followed couldn't be anything I wanted to hear. I told myself to keep control, no matter what. "I'm listening."

"I know you think I like Ellen again, but that's not the problem. I just don't like what I see happening to us since she's been back. Going together with you has been great most of the time—don't get me wrong. But I don't think I'm ready for the kind of relationship you want. I need more freedom. I don't want to have to answer to you or worry about it if what I'm doing is hurting your feelings. Do you understand?"

Understand? All I could understand was that Lenny had been my boyfriend, and it had been wonderful. But now he obviously didn't want it that way anymore. How could he expect me to feel but hurt?

It was hard for me to say anything. I was so afraid I would start to cry. "Y-you mean you want to break up, don't you?"

He swallowed hard. "I think it's better for us to go our separate ways now, Linda. Before we really hurt one another."

"Okay," I said hoarsely. "If you feel that way."

Silence. He took my hand and squeezed it briefly. Then he walked down the stairs without looking back.

I wondered what he was going to say to his friends. That he had gotten rid of the burden, the girl who liked him too much? That he was now free to mess around with Ellen or any other girl?

And what was I going to say to everyone? How could I face a group of people who knew I had just been dumped?

I realized the sooner I did it, the better. I would force myself to go outside, laugh, and show everyone that none of this bothered me. The pain didn't exist. It didn't matter at all.

Chapter

Five

THE DAYS FOLLOWING our break-up were some of the worst days of my life. The pain I felt at the loss of Lenny never left me. When I was with other people, I continued to put up a front. I tried to act as if I were doing fine without Lenny, and it didn't bother me to know all his spare time was now being spent at Ellen's.

It was only when I was alone that I allowed the pain to come out. At night, in my bed, I would think of Lenny, how great it was when things were good, and I would start to cry.

I blamed myself for what had gone wrong in our relationship. If only I could have been more easygoing, if only I hadn't shown my emotions when I had felt mad or hurt or angry, if only I could have controlled my temper, if only I could take Ellen and wipe her off the face of the earth!

I would cry myself to sleep. I would dream these awful dreams of having Lenny and losing Lenny. I would wake up with this familiar knot in the pit of my stomach. Then I would start torturing myself with the "if onlys" again. I was thoroughly miserable.

Then, when things looked bleakest, they suddenly began to turn around. On Saturday morning, I awakened to the sound of my name being called. "Linda. Linda! L-liin-daaa!"

It took me a while to realize the sound wasn't my parents' voices, and it wasn't coming from inside my apartment. I sprang out of bed, ran to the window, and looked out.

There, in the street, stood a very shabby, bedraggled group. It was Sheldon, Nicky, Billy, and Lenny, all staring up at me with grins on their faces.

"What are you guys doing up so early?" I asked.

"It's not that we're up early—it's that we're out late!" Sheldon yelled up at me.

"We've been out all night," said Nicky.

"And now that the sun is up, Lenny discovered he needs his sunglasses," explained Billy.

"I left them up at your house. Can I come get them—please?" Lenny added. Those were the first words he had said to me since our break-up the week before.

"I guess," I said. "Just give me some time to get dressed."

"You don't have to—" he began. But I didn't wait to hear what he had to say. I raced into the bathroom to wash my face, comb my hair, brush my teeth, and throw on some clothes.

By the time the bell rang I was presentable. I opened the door and stood staring at Lenny.

Our eyes met and I felt that force between us, as strong as ever. How was I ever going to get over Lenny when my feelings were so intense?

He must have felt something, too, because he stared

back at me for what seemed a long time. Finally, he pulled his eyes away.

"M-my glasses," he said, remembering what he had come for.

"Glasses? Oh—uh—sure!" I got them from the dresser where I kept my things. "Here!" I held them out to him.

"Thanks." As he took them, his fingers brushed my hand. I felt this shiver travel up my arm and through my entire body. My eyes locked his again, silently pleading for him to want me like he did before. Then, afraid he would see my desperate longing, I said a quick, "Bye," and closed the door.

I leaned up against it for a moment, taking deep breaths. Seeing Lenny so close and not being able to have him was painful, there was no doubt about it. But it had showed me one thing. The attraction between us was still there, and if he felt even half the energy I did, there was still hope.

My hopes continued to grow as the last days of summer vacation slipped away. Lenny began spending less time at Ellen's and more time back at the park where he knew I would be. He gave no indication that he wanted to get back together, but there were definitely signs the interest was still there.

At first, these were just small signs. He challenged me to a game of backgammon in the park and let his fingers rest on mine each time he took the dice from me. He gave me his sweater one night when the wind began to blow and I grew chilly, then cuddled up next to me so I could keep him warm. He even made little jokes to me about breaking up, saying that he had been looking at his watch because he had told himself he was going to do it at 8:08 P.M. but didn't have the courage until 8:11.

Ordinarily, it would have made me angry to hear that, but I felt good enough now about the way things were going so I could laugh about it instead of feeling pain. On Friday night, when we were all in the pizza place, I even went so far as to play this old song in the juke box that I thought was appropriate. It was called, "Good Timing." As soon as Lenny heard it, he turned to look at me. We stared at each other and both began to laugh.

"I guess you got me on that one, Linda," he said good-naturedly.

It felt so wonderful to be sharing good feelings with Lenny again. It made me ache for the times when things were great between us. They could be that way again; I knew they could. If only he would make a move to go back together with me!

They say all good things must come to an end, and so it was with summer vacation. On Monday, I woke up knowing I was going to have to face a new year of school.

This year, I was starting ninth grade at a new school, the Bronx High School of Technology. Tech was a special school, concentrating on math, sciences, and computers. You had to take a tough test in order to get into Tech. What motivated me to try out for it last year was the fact that Tech was Louie's school, and at that time, I was crazy over Louie.

By the time I found out I made Tech, any hopes for a relationship with Louie were gone, and I really had no desire to go there. Right now, I was wishing I could go to Washington, the regular neighborhood high school, where Lenny went.

I knew my parents wouldn't even consider letting me go there. Education was the most important thing in the world to them. They were convinced it was essential for me to go to a special school.

So here I was starting a new school I didn't want to go to in the first place. To top it off the weather was miserable. It was rainy, windy, and gloomy. I had to force myself to throw my raincoat over my new school outfit, pack up my school supplies, open my umbrella, and make my way through the downpour to the subway station. I wondered if I would run into Louie in the rain.

To my surprise, not only was Louie waiting on the platform, but Lenny and Billy as well. "What are you doing here?" I gasped. "I thought you'd be on the bus for Washington by now for sure."

"There didn't seem to be any point in it," Lenny said with a grin. "Nothing happens the first day of school; it's a waste to be there. And if this storm is going to be as bad as they're forecasting, they'll probably close school early, anyhow."

"You don't know that for sure," I protested. "And if you're already cutting school on the first day, how will you ever make it through the term?"

"You worry too much, Linda," said Lenny. "Billy and I thought we'd ride out to Tech with you for a change of pace. Aren't you glad to see me?"

"I guess," I said reluctantly. I didn't want to let him know just how glad I was that he had come to my school and not Ellen's. How I wished I could go to school with him every day.

By the time we arrived at Tech, the rain was coming down harder than ever. Rumors were flying that the storm was going to turn into a hurricane, and the schools would probably close early.

Lenny and Billy decided to go to a nearby diner to get some breakfast. "We'll hang out here for another hour or so," Lenny said. "If you can get out of school early enough, meet us here and we'll spend the day together."

"Lenny! You know I don't cut school," I protested.

"Just check it out. We'll be here waiting."

There was no way I could have concentrated on school once I knew Lenny was so close by and waiting for me. I went to my homeroom to pick up my schedule and sat there, torn, deciding what I should do.

There were eight girls in my homeroom class and thirty boys. None of the boys interested me at all. They were all so young looking, so immature. Not like Lenny, with his air of sophistication and his dynamic personality. How I longed to be with him right now.

And Lenny was right, there wasn't much going on in school on the first day. No sooner had I gotten my schedule then the announcement came that, due to the storm, classes would be shortened to ten minutes each.

That clinched it for me. As soon as the bell rang to change classes, I headed for a side door I had noticed and snuck outside. Opening my umbrella, I ran the entire way to the diner. Lenny and Billy were still there.

Lenny gave me his most charming smile. "I had a feeling you might show up. Are you prepared for the best first day of school you ever had?"

The idea of a hurricane put Billy in an adventurous mood. When we got back to Washington Heights, he wanted to walk down the drive by the river to see what the Hudson looked like in a storm. Personally, I thought he was crazy, but Lenny agreed that it would be fun. We decided to go down by the river and then come back to Lenny's house for the rest of the afternoon.

At first it was exciting, and a challenge, battling the winds and whipping rain. Once we reached the river, however, I saw my initial instincts were right. The river was high and churned by angry waves, and the rocks that led to it were wet and slippery. My raincoat and umbrella were doing nothing to keep me from getting wet, and I was also starting to get cold.

"Let's go home," I said to Lenny. He got Billy to agree, but as we started the long climb back, Billy spotted something that had washed up on the rocks.

"It's part of a wrecked boat," he announced. "And there's a fire extinguisher in it. I always wanted a fire extinguisher for my room. I'm going to get it!"

"Billy, don't! You'll get hurt!" Lenny and I yelled at him. But either the wind carried our words away or Billy wasn't listening. He picked his way over the wet rocks to where the wreck was grounded. He was fine until he reached for the fire extinguisher. Then he lost his footing and slipped. As we watched in horror, a large wave rose up and swept over him.

"Billy!" As I screamed his name, Lenny was already starting across the rocks to go to his assistance. I was terrified. What if Lenny were to slip as well? There was no way I could pull both him and Billy out of the river!

The wave receded, and it was only then that I could see it hadn't taken Billy with it. He clung to the piece of boat and managed to pull himself to his feet. By the time Lenny reached him he had gotten the extinguisher out of the boat. Lenny helped him out, and they started back across the rocks together.

"Lenny, Lenny! Are you okay? You could have been killed out there with that crazy jerk!" I ran to him anxiously as soon as he set foot on shore. I was so glad to see him safe that I threw my arms around him. I totally forgot that we were no longer going together and I had no right to do that.

Lenny seemed to have forgotten, too. He put his arms around me and held me to him. "You really care, don't you?" he murmured into my hair.

I looked at him, soaking wet, hair plastered to his forehead, water running down his face in streams. He looked so vulnerable, so adorable. I had no choice but to tell him the truth. "Yes, I do."

"Then what do you say we give it one more try?" he said softly.

"One more try," I whispered back, my heart soaring.

He kissed me, and I forgot all about the cold, hard rain beating down upon us. Lenny and I were together again. It was all that mattered.

Lenny and I spent a long time talking that day. Billy decided to take his precious fire extinguisher home, so Lenny and I went alone to his house to dry off. He gave me some of his old clothes to wear while he tossed our things into the dryer.

I felt really close to him as we sat in the kitchen drinking mugs of hot chocolate and talking about how we felt about going together and breaking up.

Lenny swore he didn't break up with me because he liked Ellen. He was just confused about how he felt, and he needed the time and freedom to find out that it was me he wanted for sure. His friends had teased him for spending so much time with me, and he was always worrying about what my reactions would be to the things he did.

I told him I didn't want to tie him down and keep him from doing things he enjoyed. I only needed to know that he cared about me, thought about my feelings, and put me before other girls.

By the time our clothes were dry, we had reached a greater understanding. This time we were determined to do it right.

The hardest part about going back with Lenny was breaking the news to my parents. They had been overjoyed when we had broken up and gone out of their way to be nice to me. Once they knew we were back together the tensions started up again.

I knew the only way things could improve was if my parents got to know Lenny better. I wanted them to see he was really intelligent and had a serious side.

I got Lenny to agree to come up to my house in the evenings and do homework with me. This would serve several purposes. I could get my homework done and still be with Lenny; he would be forced to do his own homework, and my parents could see how studious he was capable of being.

I had warned Lenny ahead of time to be extra polite to my parents. They were big on little niceties like saying hello and goodbye.

I knew it was hard for Lenny to bring himself to say anything to my parents. After all, the last thing my father had said to him was never to go near me again. It had to be uncomfortable for Lenny just to set foot in my house.

To give Lenny credit, he handled it well. He went right to the kitchen, where my parents were playing a game of Scrabble, and said, "Hello, Mr. Berman. Hello, Mrs. Berman. Thank you for letting me come here to do homework with Linda. Everyone in the neighborhood knows what a good student she is."

"And our concern is that she remain a good student," my father pointed out gruffly. I didn't think that was called for, but it was definitely an improvement over his last conversation with Lenny, so I didn't say anything.

"Naturally." Lenny refused to let my father get to him. "And it's my concern as well. That's why Linda and I have agreed to do homework together whenever possible. It'll be beneficial to us both."

There was nothing my parents could say to object to this. My mother even forced a little smile before she told us, "You can work in Ira and Joey's room. They finished their homework earlier, so they can watch TV in the living room and won't disturb you. Be sure to work at the table—and sit on chairs, not the beds!"

"Table and chairs," Lenny laughed as we left the kitchen. "Your parents are something else."

"I know," I laughed back. "But you did a great job handling them, Lenny. You said exactly what they wanted to hear. And as long as they let you up here to do homework, I don't care if we sit on the floor!"

It was a lot harder than I thought it would be to concentrate on my homework with Lenny sitting there next to me. I would answer a question, then look over at him to make sure he was really there. I had to force my mind back to my homework at least a dozen times before I finally got it done.

Lenny had finished his history but was still struggling with Spanish. He looked at me with an expression of utter frustration. "There's no way I'm going to get this verb stuff. All this nonsense about first, second, and third person, about singulars and plurals. And these ridiculous tenses with names like present indicative and past perfect. Why do they make it so darn complicated?"

I couldn't help laughing. "It's not that complicated,

Lenny. English has the same tenses, you know. We don't bother thinking about it most of the time because we're so used to speaking, but the principles are still the same. Here, let me show you."

I used the verb *to be* and explained all the tenses for that verb. Then I showed him the same thing with the Spanish verb *estar*.

"Oh, now I understand what you're doing," he said. "How come my teachers never explained it that way?"

"Maybe they did and you weren't listening, or maybe you weren't even there that day—you do cut too much, you know."

"I know," he admitted. "But school is so darn boring! Teachers talk about stuff like conjugating verbs and dissecting angles—things that have absolutely no relevance to my life. Sometimes I sit in the classroom listening to all that nonsense, and I feel as if I'm going out of my mind. It's pure torture. I have to get out of there—I just have to!"

I looked at him in surprise. Doing well in school came so easily to me that I didn't realize anyone could feel that way. "I'm sorry it's so hard for you, Lenny. I know there's a lot of stuff in school that seems irrelevant, but I bet you'd find some of it is pretty interesting if you gave it a chance. Maybe it would help if you looked at it as sort of a game we have to play. We put up with the lousy teachers and boring classes now, and we win in the long run. It's not so hard if you play by the rules—come to class, listen to what the teachers tell you to do; keep up with your assignments. It's only a matter of self-discipline."

"Well, I guess you've got more self-discipline than I do."

"Maybe—when it comes to school." I put my hand

on his. "But when it comes to you I've got absolutely none!"

He squeezed my hand and gave me a smile. "You know, you're great, Linda. There's no other girl with the depth you have. Sometimes I think I actually love you!"

Startled, I gazed into his eyes. Lenny had said he thought he loved me. But how did he mean it? Was he saying it because he was impressed with things I did well like being successful in school or being a good listener when he talked about his problems? Or was he talking about real romantic love, the kind that grown-ups felt for one another?

I felt that strange power, that special closeness, rising between us. Maybe it really was the beginnings of love. "I think I love you, too," I whispered.

Chapter

Six

LOVE. IT MADE MY HEAD SPIN to think of it. Could I really and truly love Lenny? I wasn't even sure what love meant.

I looked the word up in the dictionary. It said, "the profoundly tender and passionate feeling for a person of the opposite sex." That didn't help me much. I did feel profoundly tender and passionate for Lenny. But I knew love had to mean more than that.

To me, love meant caring for the other person. Caring so much that you might even put his needs before your own. Love meant wanting him so much that it was better to be with him, doing nothing, than to do the most exciting thing in the world with someone else.

That's the way it was with Lenny and me. We could be happy doing the silliest little things together. We would walk in the park and try to find the prettiest autumn leaves. We would sit in the back of the candy store sharing a soda and reading comic books. We would sit in the pizza place and watch the people go by in the street. We would watch TV in my living room, holding hands and ignoring the wise-guy comments my brothers kept making. We could be happy anywhere, just talking or gazing into each other's eyes.

During school, I would find myself daydreaming about Lenny. I would discover I had written his name or drawn his face all over my notebook instead of taking notes. I had to force myself to concentrate on what the teacher was saying.

As soon as school was over, I would race home to see him. During the afternoon we would usually hang around the candy store or go up to someone's house with the other kids from the crowd. At night, it became a ritual for Lenny and I to do homework together.

I thought this was the perfect way to get Lenny to start doing well in school again. When he was younger and could get by through brains alone, he had always gotten good grades. But high school was much harder, and he couldn't seem to buckle down and do the work. He said it was hard for him to concentrate at home because he was always fighting with his mother. I figured having him study with me would solve the problem.

It was very important to me that Lenny do well in school. I kept checking up on him and asking questions to make sure he was doing the right thing. Stuff like, "How did school go today?" and "You went to all your classes today, didn't you?"

He would answer that school was as boring as ever, but he was going to his classes and doing much better.

I believed him and thought all was well. Then came that day in mid-October when a group of us was hanging around the candy store after school as usual. It was one of those dreary New York days when the clouds were heavy and the rain would drizzle down, stop, then start up again. Each time it started, we would huddle under the candy store awning, trying not to get wet. It was cold and miserable, and no one seemed to come up with anything to do.

"Why don't we go up to your house, Billy?" Donna finally suggested. "Your mother will be home from work soon, and she doesn't usually mind having us there."

"No, she doesn't," Billy admitted. "Except for Lenny, that is."

I saw Lenny flash him a dirty look when he said this, and was filled with a sense of apprehension. Something was going on I didn't know about.

"Why doesn't your mother want Lenny at your house, Billy?" I asked.

"Well—uh—you know. She sort of doesn't think some of the things he's been doing are cool. You know what I mean?"

"No. I don't know what you mean. What things are you talking about?"

"Well—uh—like—uh—" Billy looked at Lenny and saw his angry glare. "Look, why don't you just ask Lenny?"

I did. "What's going on here that I don't know about, Lenny?"

Lenny's face blushed red. "It's nothing. Mrs. Upton got a bit upset about a little incident that happened at school, that's all. She blamed me and decided she doesn't want me at her house anymore."

"Oh. And what was this 'little incident'?"

Lenny squirmed. "Well, it had to do with school. Mrs. Upton is blaming me for some classes Billy cut— but she's wrong, of course."

"Yeah," agreed Billy. "I don't need Lenny to cut. I can cut by myself any time I want."

"But this time you cut *with* Lenny, right?" I demanded.

"Well, uh—yeah." Billy admitted. "But why not? Biology lab's a real drag. We had to do it for our own sanity. Didn't we, Lip?" He looked to Lenny.

But Lenny was looking at me, probably trying to assess just how angry I was at hearing this.

I was plenty angry. Lenny had promised me he was going to stop cutting classes and get serious about school. I now knew he and Billy had cut together yesterday. I couldn't help wondering how many times he had cut that I hadn't found out about. I asked him, trying without much success to keep the anger out of my voice.

He looked hurt. "Why, Linda, how could you accuse me of something like that? I promised you I wouldn't cut, and I don't. This was just something unfortunate that came up."

"Oh yeah? Like what?"

"Like why don't we go up to Billy's, and I'll explain the whole thing to you."

"But what about Billy's mother?" I asked. "She doesn't want you at her house."

"I'll explain it to her, too." Lenny laughed. "I've known Mrs. Upton a long time. I know how to charm her!"

Not only did Lenny know how to charm Mrs. Upton; he also knew how to charm me. By the time both of us had heard his story, we couldn't be angry at him anymore.

Mrs. Upton started to protest when she saw him, but he calmed her right down by apologizing for Billy's having gotten into trouble and requesting the chance to explain what had happened. We sat in the living room while Lenny told his tale of woe.

"My mother and I have been fighting more than ever recently," he began. "Now that I've turned sixteen, she decided she's not going to do anything for me anymore. She expects me to buy my own food, do my own laundry, earn my own money, and take care of myself in general. Well, yesterday morning I got up too late to get anything for breakfast, and there was nothing to eat in the house. I made it through the first two periods of school okay, but by the time I got to Bio Lab I was so hungry I thought I was going to pass out. I knew I couldn't last until lunch, and I was too sick to be able to concentrate on class anyhow. Billy noticed the horrible state I was in and suggested I should get something to eat immediately. He even offered to walk with me to Hershey's Diner to make sure I was okay. That's the kind of son you have, Mrs. Upton. Not everyone would have been willing to sacrifice Bio Lab to help a sick friend. He never considered the fact he might get into trouble for being there for me—he just did it out of the goodness of his heart. You should be proud of Billy, not angry at him."

By the time Lenny had finished his story, my eyes were brimming with tears. I felt guilty for having gotten angry at him before I knew the facts about what had happened. Poor Lenny was neglected by his mother. How could anyone expect a growing boy with his appetite to get through a day of school without any food? It was absolutely cruel!

Apparently, Mrs. Upton thought so, too. "That's terrible about your mother, Lenny. Perhaps I should speak to her about the problem?"

"Oh no, Mrs. Upton. I couldn't have you get involved. My mother probably would wind up getting angry at you for interfering, and it wouldn't do any good, anyhow. No, I'll just look for a job after school so I can earn enough money to pay for my groceries and expenses. And I'll be sure to eat in the morning so I don't get sick in school."

"That's right, Lenny. I'm always telling Billy not to skip breakfast," said Mrs. Upton. "Now, if this ever happens again and you find yourself without food in the morning, remember that you're welcome to come up here and have breakfast with us!" Mrs. Upton smiled sympathetically at Lenny, then excused herself to the kitchen so she could start preparing dinner.

"Boy, did she change her tune fast," commented Fran when Mrs. Upton left.

"Yeah, she really fell for Lenny's story," said Donna. "And so did you, didn't you, Linda?"

"Why don't you shut up and mind your own business, Donna?" Lenny said hotly. "Why shouldn't Linda believe me—I'm telling the truth."

"Come on, Donna," I said. "No one would make up a story like that. Of course I believe Lenny."

But even as I said this, there was part of me that was not comfortable with this situation. Even if everything Lenny had said was true, there had to have been a better way to handle things without cutting school. Once he got into the habit of cutting again, it could easily lead to more cutting, and soon he could be in danger of failing his classes.

I shook the thought out of my mind and cuddled up next to Lenny on the sofa. I would give him the benefit of the doubt this time. I really did want to believe he was sincere about school.

Two weeks later, I found out that Lenny cut again. One of his friends, Chris Berland, had helped Lenny get a job in City Drugs, a pharmacy where Chris had once worked. The job was from six till ten, Monday through Thursday, which meant we could no longer study together those nights. Still, I was glad that Lenny had the job because I knew he needed the money.

One day I saw Chris in the street and decided to thank him for getting the job for Lenny. During our conversation, Chris let it slip that he and Lenny had cut history together, and more than once.

I got this sick feeling when he said that. The fear that Lenny would start slipping in school once we were no longer studying together had entered my mind before, but I had put it out again. I had wanted to believe that he would be okay once I had helped him back on the right track. But here was evidence that he was resuming his old habits.

Now that I had this information, I didn't know what to do with it. If I confronted Lenny, he was bound to get angry and defensive, and we would probably have a fight. If I didn't say anything, I would be eating myself up inside. I decided it would be best to say nothing and to wait and see what would happen. What happened was that once I saw him, I couldn't wait at all.

It started out innocently enough. "Why don't we go to my house this afternoon and do homework together—we haven't done that in a long time," I suggested when we met on my corner the next day.

"Why don't we go to my house and use the time for something more exciting?" he countered.

Ordinarily, I might have taken him up on his offer, or at least made a joke of it. This time, however, I was too upset by what I had learned from Chris to see anything humorous in the situation.

"That's all you ever think of, Lenny," I said hotly. "If you paid half as much attention to your schoolwork as you do to making out, you'd be better off."

"And if you paid half the attention to making out as you did to schoolwork, you'd be better off," he came right back at me.

This got me angry, and once I was angry I lost all chance of staying in control. "We'll see how far that attitude will get you in life, Lenny Lipoff! Especially when you keep cutting school!"

"School? Who says I'm cutting school?"

"Who said doesn't make any difference, Lenny. The point is that I know you've been cutting again, and you promised you wouldn't!"

"Well, I can't always run my life based on promises to you. I try not to cut, but sometimes things or circumstances come up—and . . . well, that's just the way it goes."

"Is it? Well, how come these 'circumstances' never seem to come up for me? I haven't cut school since the first day. And I haven't gotten under 90 on an exam either. So, that just goes to show you . . ."

"To show me what? That you're Miss Perfect? Whoop-dee-do! What gives you the right to tell everyone else how to live their lives? If you'd mind your own darn business, Linda, everyone would be better off for it!"

"Okay, you want me to mind my own business? I will!" I whirled around, stormed into my building, and went stomping up the steps to my apartment.

I was furious! How dare Lenny talk that way to me? I was only thinking of him, only looking out for his best interests, and he had turned on me as if I had attacked him or something.

I stayed upstairs for the rest of the afternoon, waiting for him to come up and apologize to me. It didn't happen. I guessed Lenny was as mad at me as I was at him, although I couldn't understand why. Well, I just hoped he would get over it fast, because this was Thursday, and I didn't want anything to drag on that might ruin the weekend.

All day Friday, in school, I kept thinking of my situation with Lenny. I kept looking around at the boys in my classes and comparing them to Lenny.

Every one of them was bright. Every one of them did well in school. Every one of them would go on to college and have a career as an engineer or a scientist or a doctor, lawyer, accountant, or businessman. If only I had one of these typical Tech boys for a boyfriend, I would have it made. I wouldn't have to keep after them to study and do right in school. They knew what it took to be a success in life, and they went out and did it.

Why was Lenny so different? He was as bright as any boy in Tech and twice as clever. Why couldn't he straighten up and do the right things in his life? Why couldn't he let me show him the way?

And, knowing all the problems he had, why was I so attracted to him? Why did my heart start soaring at the sound of his voice or the touch of his hand? Why did kissing him put me in this magic place where nothing else mattered? Why did I hang on every word he said as if it was the absolute truth?

I didn't have the answers to these questions. I only knew that Lenny had a stronger hold on me than I ever could have imagined. I decided I was going to have to make up with him even if he didn't apologize to me for breaking his promise and cutting. But I didn't know how to go about it.

Lenny hardly looked at me when I showed up at the candy store after school. I wouldn't look at him either. It was obvious he was still mad at me, and for what? It was he who did all the rotten things, not me. What did he expect—for me to come and apologize to him?

I stood and talked to the girls while he stood not ten feet away and talked to the boys. I was very aware of his every move, but I didn't let on. I pretended to be fascinated by Roz's discussion of what was going on in her graphic design class, and Fran and Donna's description of their new and gorgeous English teacher. But all the while, my ears were tuned into snatches of conversation that floated to me from the boys.

"Sick of hanging out—time for a change—poolroom at nine." It didn't take me long to figure out what that meant. If the boys were talking about meeting at nine, they weren't going to be taking us anywhere first. They considered the poolroom to be their own private territory. They were planning on Friday night without us.

"Listen, girls, I'm getting hungry. How about walking me into the candy store while I decide what I want?" I said this loud enough for the boys to hear.

Roz, Fran, and Donna followed me into the candy store. I ushered them quickly to the back where we couldn't be seen from the street.

"I wanted to let you know girls—I overheard some of what the boys were saying. They're meeting at the poolroom at nine, so they're obviously planning on dumping us tonight."

"Oh yeah?" said Donna. "That'll be the third Friday in a row Billy's found a reason to dump me. I'm sick of it!"

"Me, too," said Roz. "These boys have it made. They go off by themselves whenever they feel like it, and when they're in the mood for us they think all they have to do is snap their fingers and we'll be there!"

"It's true," I said glumly. "And it's disgusting. Here I'm the one with reason to be mad at Lenny, and he goes around acting as if it's all my fault. He knows exactly what to do to manipulate me. I'm sick of it!"

"I'm sick of a lot of things, too," said Fran. "Ever since Danny moved away, he's been acting as if I have nothing better to do than to sit around and wait for him to show up on weekends. Then, if there's nothing exciting planned, he doesn't even bother to come. It's ridiculous!"

"Wait a minute! I think you just hit upon the answer, Fran," I told her.

"I did? What?"

"When you said there's nothing exciting planned. That's just the problem—we're always counting on the boys for excitement. What we've got to do is show them we can make our own plans and have our own excitement, with them or without them."

"Like how?" Donna asked. "We aren't even allowed to go to exciting places like they do—like the poolroom for instance."

"But that's the whole point!" I said. "Look at that statement you just made—we're not *allowed* to go to the poolroom. Well, who's not allowing us? The boys made up that silly rule about the poolroom's being off limits to girls. There's no valid reason we can't go there if we really want to. We're entitled to as much as they are."

"Linda's right," Roz agreed. "Let's do it!"

So we girls made a pact. This would be the night we would crash the poolroom and show the boys we could do anything they could do, once and for all!

Chapter

Seven

THE EXCITEMENT WAS BUILDING as we girls walked together to the poolroom that night. We were laughing and joking and speculating on the colors the boys would turn when they found us shooting pool.

"You know, girls, this is the best time we've had together since we all acquired boyfriends," I told my friends.

"It goes to show you that boys aren't everything," said Fran. "We can have plenty of fun without them."

At that, Donna started singing some feminist song about being a woman. We all laughed and joined in with her. We linked arms and marched up the hill to the Heights poolroom, singing as loudly as we could.

People passing in the street stared at us as if we were crazy, but we didn't care. This was our big night—we girls were about to conquer the poolroom!

But when we got to the entrance, our courage faded fast. The poolroom was located above some government and social security offices, up a flight of stairs. The entrance was dark and dingy. The paint was flaking off the walls, and a rancid odor permeated the air.

"Phew—this place stinks!" Roz wrinkled her nose. "Are you sure you really want to go up there, Linda?"

I wasn't, but I didn't want to say that. After all, this had been my idea. As I was wondering how to handle this one, I spotted Chris Berland coming up the street. My answer had been sent to me!

Chris was big and Chris was strong. Chris was always nice to girls. He was the perfect person to escort us up to the poolroom and show us how things were done up there.

"Hi, Chris!" I bounded up to him and gave him my biggest smile. "You wouldn't be heading up to the poolroom by any chance, would you?"

"Yeah, I am," he said.

"Well, we girls were just heading up there ourselves. Since it's our first time, we were hoping you—well, uh—we'd like you to—uh, would you—uh?"

"Show you around?" Chris finished my sentence and grinned.

"Yeah," I grinned back in relief. I knew Chris was the right one to ask.

We followed his muscular body up the steps. "After you, ladies." He held the door for us and we filed in to the infamous male stronghold we had been curious about for so long.

What we saw was worse than I thought it would be. Pool tables stretched in two long rows down either side of an aisle, and the only lighting was from flourescent fixtures directly over each table. Deep shadows took over the rest of the room, creating a dark, furtive, and sinister atmosphere that made me shiver. The awful smell was stronger here, as it originated from two bathrooms located near the entranceway. A thick haze of smoke filled the air and made it difficult to breathe without choking. And the sound of men laughing and cursing and of balls clattering was so loud it hurt my ears.

"Ugh," said fastidious Roz. "Let's get out of here!"

"We can't," I told her. "We're here for a reason. If the boys find out we chickened out and ran when we got here, we'll never live it down."

"She's right," said Fran, who can be nuttier than I can. Her support gave me the courage I needed.

"Chris, what do we have to do to get to play?" I asked.

"Go up to the desk and ask Charlie to assign you a table and clock your time," he said. "Then come back here, pick out your cues, and start to play."

"Will you show us how—I mean the finer points of the game?" I was a bit embarrassed to admit that none of us knew the first thing about how to shoot pool.

"Sure," he grinned. "It'll give me some time to sharpen my skills before the guys get here."

That's how Chris came to demonstrate to us the basics of the game of pool. You made a bridge with the fingers of one hand and rested the long cue on it. You figured out what angle the ball you wanted to get into the pocket needed to be hit at in order to get it there. Then you aimed the white ball so it would hit the other ball at that angle. You took your shot and hoped for the best.

The game was a lot harder than it looked. If you didn't hit it right, the ball could go wild all over the table. Or even worse, you could miss and scratch up the green felt table covering. The game required a lot of concentration.

I take my games very seriously. It's a carryover

from when I was younger and a tomboy and had to prove I was as good in sports as the boys were. So I was concentrating carefully when it was my turn to try to hit the number three ball into the corner pocket.

I was concentrating so hard that I was unaware the boys had entered the poolroom. I was unaware of the shocked and angry expressions on their faces when they saw us there. I was unaware they had come over and surrounded the table, and were watching me take aim for my shot. And I was unaware that Lenny was standing behind me.

I took my shot. The white ball connected with the three ball almost exactly where I wanted it to. Click! The ball landed right in the pocket.

"All right!" I yelled triumphantly and looked around for approval. When I saw who was there the words froze right in my throat. My friends looked pale and frightened; the boys looked angry, and Chris looked amused. But it wasn't until I saw the look on Lenny's face that I realized the full impact of what was happening. He was absolutely furious!

"W-what do you think you're doing here?" he sputtered.

"P-playing pool," I said simply.

"Didn't I tell you—" he began. Then off he went into a tirade about how the poolroom was the boys' special place and they didn't want a bunch of girls spoiling it for them. As he spoke, he got himself angrier and angrier. His face got red and the veins in his neck stood out—a sure sign he had lost his temper.

Donna, at least, was not afraid of Lenny. "Why don't you shut up, Lenny? We didn't come here to listen to your mouth."

"Oh yeah? What did you come up here for, then?" Billy brought his face real close to hers and growled.

That quieted Donna down fast. She might not have been afraid of Lenny, but Billy had her right where he wanted her.

"Might I remind you, Billy, that we have as much right to be here as you do," I said. "We came here to learn to shoot pool, and we intend to stay here until we do!"

"Or until our hour is up, which may come first," Fran tried to inject a little humor.

The boys were not amused. They gathered around us as if we were some sort of criminals. Of course Lenny was the only one who came up with an ultimatum. "If you don't get out of here right now, Linda, that's it for us. We're through!"

I stared at him in disbelief. Could he be serious? It was true we hadn't been getting along the past few days, but most of the time our relationship had been great. Lenny had told me that he loved me and how wonderful I made him feel. Could he really mean he would break up with me if I didn't do what he demanded? I couldn't believe that of him.

"That's ridiculous, Lenny. All we're doing is shooting some pool. We're not hurting you in any way."

"Oh no?" He came over and grabbed my arm. "Well, let me tell you something, Linda. I don't like having any girl I'm associated with seen in a sleazy place like this. If you don't care about your own self-respect, it's bad enough. But if you don't care about my feelings and embarrassing me, that's it as far as I'm concerned. So, make up your mind. Would you rather shoot pool or have me for a boyfriend?"

Of course I would rather have Lenny, but something inside me refused to give in to his threats. I didn't think Lenny had any right to be embarrassed by what I was doing. I had as much right to be in the poolroom as he did. I had gotten the girls to come up here, and I wasn't going to lose face in front of them and the boys, too.

"Let go of me," was all I said, pulling away from his grasp. Then I walked around the table to find the best angle for my next shot.

"Okay, Linda, have it your way. It's over!" He spit out the words. "Come on, guys. Let's get out of here!" With a last glare at Donna and Roz, Billy and Sheldon followed Lenny out of the poolroom.

We girls finished our game, but all the fun had gone out of the evening for us. We went for ice cream sundaes to try to cheer ourselves up.

I couldn't eat mine. I stared at the mound of whipped cream piled over the strawberry ice cream and syrup, and pushed it around with my spoon.

"Come on, Linda. It's not so bad," Fran tried to comfort me. "Lenny was just angry. I bet he didn't mean it about breaking up."

"Sheldon and Billy were angry, too," I pointed out. "But they didn't break up with Roz and Donna."

"That's because Lenny is a hothead," said Roz. "And truthfully, so are you. Both of you want to prove something, to get the best of one another."

"Roz, how can you say that?" I asked. "I wasn't trying to get the best of Lenny. The only thing I wanted to prove was that we girls can have fun on our own and do whatever we want to, the same as the boys can. And that includes going to the poolroom."

"Well, I think you did prove that," said Fran. "We were having fun until the boys showed up."

"But is it worth the price we're paying?" asked Donna. "The boys could decide to stay mad at us forever."

"I don't think so," said Roz. "They'll quiet down

once they realize we're right. Even Lenny, Linda. I'm sure he's not going to really break up with you over something silly like this."

I took heart at what Roz said. I couldn't believe Lenny would break up with me over something silly like this, either.

The next day was sunny and warm for late October, and I knew everyone would be out at the park taking advantage of the Indian summer. It was the kind of day I loved best. I would have been feeling wonderful if it wasn't for this ball of fear sitting in my stomach, fear of what might happen when I saw Lenny.

He wasn't at the wall when I arrived. Ellen wasn't there either. I couldn't help wondering if they were together somewhere. As the afternoon wore on with no sign of either Lenny or Ellen, the fear kept growing. I had to find out the truth.

I cornered Sheldon and asked him to take a walk with me. Roz had been right about him, at least. He was no longer angry about the poolroom. He seemed perfectly willing to talk about Lenny.

"He went to New Jersey with his mother to visit his aunt and uncle," Sheldon told me. "He said he probably would be gone all day."

"That doesn't sound like Lenny," I said suspiciously. "He doesn't get along with his mother. Why would he go with her to visit his aunt and uncle?"

"This is his favorite aunt and uncle. Besides, they had a belated birthday gift to give him, so he wanted to go get it."

"Oh. Now *that* sounds like Lenny!" I couldn't help laughing. I made the decision to be open with Sheldon. After all, he had been the one to get Lenny and me together in the first place. "What do you think, Sheldon? Was Lenny serious about breaking up with me last night?"

"Well, I don't know how serious he was. But he was plenty angry."

"But why? Don't you think we girls have a right to go to the poolroom if we want to? Pool isn't a game that's only for boys!"

"Well, if you're really interested in learning the game, the bowling alley has pool tables. So do a lot of other places where the atmosphere is nice. It's just this poolroom that we object having you come to. I guess we want to look at it as ours."

"But why?" I asked again.

"Because it's a fact that boys have certain needs apart from their girlfriends. We need a place to go to be with each other, a place where we can cut loose, let off some steam, and just be one of the boys. We like to look at the poolroom as our place to go to when we feel like that. It's nothing personal against you girls; it's just the way things are. And it's probably something you're going to have to accept, Linda—if you want your relationship with Lenny to work out."

I thought a lot about what Sheldon had said because I did want my relationship with Lenny to work out. What if Sheldon was right and Lenny did need the poolroom to go to to let off steam and be one of the boys? I could understand that because there were times we girls needed to be by ourselves, too. If I tried to stop Lenny, he could only wind up resenting me for it. And I didn't even like the sleazy old poolroom anyhow. It probably was better to let the boys have it for their own.

Sunday was another beautiful day, and our crowd had arranged to go to Central Park together for a game of co-ed football. I was hoping Lenny would be among the kids who gathered at the wall, but he wasn't. Neither was Ellen.

This time Sheldon didn't know where Lenny might be. "He knew about the game today. He was supposed to show up," was all he could tell me.

Once at the park, I tried to keep my mind on the game, but it was hard for me to do. I kept thinking about Lenny and whether he was with Ellen. Besides, the game wasn't a very good one. The boys were so much bigger, stronger, and faster than the girls were. They kept passing the ball to each other and hardly gave us a chance to do anything. It was frustrating.

I had no patience for this kind of thing today. I was considering quitting the game and going off for a walk by myself, when Roz elbowed me in my side. "Look, Linda. Isn't that Lenny approaching?"

I looked and saw it was. I could tell his body that seemed to be getting taller each day and his bouncy walk, even from a distance. My first reaction was to be glad he had showed up without Ellen. Then I was filled with fear at how he might react to me, and I was tempted to run away. But I couldn't—not in front of everyone in the crowd.

I hung back uncomfortably on the outskirts of the group that went over to greet Lenny. He didn't even look at me and I was sure he was still angry.

Chris, who was the organizer of the game, assigned Lenny a position on the opposite team. This was good because I wouldn't have to get too close to him if I was careful. Also, it was motivation for me to start paying attention to the game. With Lenny on the enemy team, there was nothing I wanted more than to make some outstanding play that would enable our side to win.

I saw my chance when Chris threw a pass meant for Sheldon. Danny managed to knock him out of the way. There was no one in position to catch the ball, but I was close. I took off running, trying to intercept the ball before it reached the ground.

I ran as fast as I could, watching the ball the whole time. I could do it—I knew I could. I reached out both arms to grab the ball, then—whack! I ran into someone who had the same idea I did.

The impact caused me to fall forward and land on my stomach. The person I had collided with fell on top of me with enough force so I lost my breath. The ball bounced away, and neither of us could get it.

"Get off of me!" Angrily, I rolled over and pushed away the person who had kept me from my moment of glory. I almost died when I saw it was Lenny.

"You—you made me miss the ball!" I sputtered.

"Naturally—that's the point!" he grinned. "After all, you're not on my team!"

It was then I noticed there was blood on his mouth. "Oh, your lip—it's bleeding!" Without thinking, I reached out to touch it.

"Is it? Where?" He placed his hand on top of mine.

Then I became aware that everyone had gathered around us. "Are you okay?" they were saying. "Where did all that blood come from?"

"It's just my lip." Lenny pulled my hand away.

"Better go wash it off," suggested Roz. "It could get all infected if you've got dirt in it."

"Yeah, I guess I will." Lenny picked himself up from the ground and brushed himself off. "I passed a water fountain on my way to the field. You're full of blood, too, Linda. Want to come?"

Did I want to come? My heart started beating so fast when he said that, I was afraid everyone would hear. "Well, I guess I should." I tried to sound as if I didn't really care.

"We're going to have to go on with the game without you," Chris warned as we left.

"That's okay," Lenny said. I was glad. So he wasn't that interested in the game either.

We walked to the fountain in silence. I certainly didn't know what to say to him, and for once he didn't seem to know what to say to me. When we got there I rinsed off my hands. He took water in his mouth, swished it around, and spat it on the ground.

"How's my lip?"

I examined it carefully. "A little swollen. And there's still some dirt in it. If you have a tissue or something, I'll get it off for you."

He pulled a handkerchief out of his pocket and handed it to me. It didn't look overly clean, but I took it just the same. I rinsed it with water and dabbed his lip.

"Ow! Careful! You're brutal!" he complained.

"Not as brutal as you are!" I came right back at him.

We stood there glaring at each other for a moment, then he began to laugh. "You know, you look awfully cute when you're angry, Linda. The trouble is you're angry much too often!"

"Me? What about you?" I demanded. But I couldn't stay angry long when Lenny was laughing.

We started walking back toward the game together. Then Lenny suggested that since it was such a nice day and the game was doing fine without us, we ought to walk around the park and have a little talk.

"Okay," I agreed. My heart was pounding again. What was he going to say?

At first he kept the conversation light. We talked

about how beautiful the park looked in autumn, which was Lenny's favorite time of the year. He showed me the gift his aunt and uncle had given him, a beautiful gold ring with an *L* on it for his name. I didn't let him know how happy I was to find he really was at his aunt's and not with Ellen or some other girl.

We sat on a rock that overlooked the playing field, far enough away so we could watch the game without being seen ourselves. The sky was a crisp blue which accentuated the colors of the turning leaves. Soft, white puffs of clouds drifted by, forming ever-changing shapes that were fascinating to watch. It was wonderful to be with Lenny on this beautiful day. I could pretend that the fight between us had never happened.

"Look at that cloud—it looks just like a swan drifting on a lake!" I pointed to the sky.

He looked where I was pointing. "Hey, you're right. I see it, too. And look, over there . . . that looks like a kitten!"

"It does! And there's a ball of twine for it to play with!"

He looked at me. "You know, it's hard to believe the soft, calm Linda I see today is the same person I saw so stubbornly planting herself in the poolroom the other night."

The smile faded from my face. "And it's hard to believe that this sweet, loving Lenny is the same person who became a raving lunatic just to see me there."

I felt myself growing angry again, but then I thought of what Sheldon had told me. Maybe the boys really did need the poolroom for a place to go off to on their own. "Well, Lenny, I'll tell you one thing. You don't have to worry about having me come up to the poolroom anymore. And not because you scared me away, either. That place is disgusting. You boys can have it all to yourselves if that's the way you want it."

"Good! Because that *is* the way we want it."

"Fine, then it's settled," I said, in a completely non-combative way.

I guess my attitude surprised him, because the next thing he said was totally unexpected. "I guess I owe you an apology for the way I exploded the other night, Linda. I was so angry to find you where I didn't want you to be, that I lost sight of the fact that you really did have a right to be there."

I took a deep breath. "I think you hit upon the answer, Lenny. We both have to remember that because we're boyfriend and girlfriend, it doesn't mean we can tell the other person what to do. We're each entitled to make our own decisions and do what we want, as long as we're not hurting the other person."

"I agree. Especially since you've told me that going to the poolroom is something you don't want to do any longer," he said with his cocky grin.

"I don't, I don't," I promised. "That is, for as long as we're going together. We are still going together, aren't we?"

"Of course!" He put his arm around me. "After all, who else could I spend a day with looking for animals in the clouds? In fact, there's a big whale spouting water, right now!"

"Whale? Where?"

"Just turn your head a little—this way!"

I turned toward him, and as I did, he kissed me on the lips. I kissed him back, and I felt wonderful. This was one difficult situation we had managed to come through together.

During the weeks that followed, I really made an effort to let Lenny do what he wanted, as long as it wasn't something that would hurt me. I tried not to bother him about things like school and homework.

It paid off. On November 26, the four-month anniversary of the day we started going together, he asked me to wear his new ring on a chain around my neck. That meant we were officially going steady.

I was elated. Not that I thought going steady would make much difference. Lenny and I saw each other almost every day anyhow, and neither of us was dating anyone else. But the fact he wanted me to wear his ring was proof that he really cared.

Chapter
_____
Eight

GOING STEADY seemed to be good for Lenny and me. We got along well and were together as much as possible.

Christmas vacation arrived, and everyone was talking about what to do on New Year's Eve. Most of the kids thought it would be nice to have a party, but no one seemed to be able to have it in their house. As New Year's approached, it looked as if there was going to be nothing to do.

In the meanwhile, Mrs. Faine, the lady whose kids I had been baby-sitting for recently, was putting pressure on me to sit for her on New Year's. She and her husband wanted to get theater tickets, but since I was their only hope for a babysitter, if I couldn't sit for them, they couldn't go.

I told Mrs. Faine I would let her know in time to get the tickets. Every day I asked Lenny if we were going to do anything.

"New Year's is a horrible time to go out," he said. "Everything's crowded and expensive, and people are drunk and acting crazy. I don't want to go out. If we don't get a party going somewhere, we probably won't do anything."

Two days before New Year's Eve, nothing had materialized. "I guess I'll tell Mrs. Faine I'll sit for her," I told Lenny. "She's been really nice to me and given me a lot of work to do. She even gave me a present for Christmas. I owe it to her to baby-sit."

"You owe it to yourself to do what you want to do," he said. "You don't have to baby-sit on New Year's if you don't want to."

"But there doesn't seem to be anything going on anyway."

"No," he admitted. "But you never can tell what might develop at the last minute."

Nothing had developed by the time Mrs. Faine called me that evening, so I told her I would baby-sit. Wouldn't you know it, the next day, someone came up with a place for a party. Jessie Scaley, this girl who had recently been dating Louie, got her mother to agree to a party. Everyone who hung out on the park wall or the candy store was invited. It was going to be the event of the year.

"And now I'm stuck baby-sitting!" I complained to my mother. "I can't believe it. All along there was nothing to do. Then, as soon as I told Mrs. Faine I would sit, this comes up. It's not fair!"

"You can't back out now, Linda. Mr. Faine already picked up the tickets."

"I know," I said glumly. "I wouldn't do that to them. It's just that I'm going to be so miserable thinking of everyone having a great time at Jessie's while I'm stuck by myself watching TV."

My mother could see how unhappy I was. I guess she felt sorry for me. At any rate, she did something really unexpected. She volunteered to take over my baby-sitting for part of the night so I could spend some time at the party.

"I'll come from ten until one," she said. "I don't want to have to put the kids to bed or be out late myself. But that should give you the best hours at the party."

"Oh it will—thanks, Ma!" I went over and hugged her. This was the nicest thing my mother had done for me since I had started going with Lenny. I was really grateful.

I didn't know then that I would have been better off if I had never set foot in that party at all.

Jessie's party was well under way by the time I got there. It was crowded with kids—all of whom I knew from the neighborhood. My closest friends were there—Roz, Fran, and Donna. So were some girls we could have done without, but who were good friends with Jessie—Ellen, whom I still didn't trust near Lenny, Kathy Jones, who was nice but seemed to have designs on Sheldon, and Renee, who flirted more than ever since she had stopped going with Louie.

The boys included: Danny, Sheldon, Billy, Louie, Chris, Nicky, and of course, Lenny. There was also this new boy, Tony Hall, who had started hanging around with us recently, as he had gotten friendly with Sheldon. I wasn't sure how I felt about Tony. He lived in a neighborhood that was tougher than ours, and you could tell it by the way he talked and acted. Sometimes he scared me, but he did try hard to be accepted. Lenny had decided right away he didn't like Tony, but I thought it was only fair to give him a chance.

The first thing I saw when I arrived at the party was that Lenny was dancing with Ellen. Even though

Lenny and I had an agreement we could both dance with whomever we wanted at parties, it didn't make me happy to find him with her. It put me in a bad mood from the start.

I busied myself talking to my friends and getting some snacks to eat, all the time watching Lenny to see what he would do. I don't know if he noticed I was there or not, but he wound up dancing the next dance with Renee.

Now I was doubly angry. So, when Tony came over and asked me to dance, I didn't stop to think about how he sometimes scared me. I went and danced.

Now I was sure Lenny saw me. He looked at me in Tony's arms and scowled. This got me angry. That was some greeting from my boyfriend on New Year's Eve!

When the dance was over, he came over and steered me into the kitchen, which was empty. "Why did you have to go and dance with Tony as soon as you arrived at the party?" he demanded. "I told you he was no good."

I didn't like his attitude. "For your information, Lenny, I hadn't just arrived at the party. "If you weren't so busy drooling over Ellen and Renee, you might have noticed!"

"Well, if you hadn't made those dumb baby-sitting arrangements, maybe I would have been dancing with you instead. What did you expect me to do, sit in a corner until you showed up?"

"No. But you knew I was going to be here by ten-fifteen. You could have at least been interested enough to look for me!"

All this time our voices kept rising in intensity. Renee came in for some ice cubes and interrupted us.

"Ooops! Excuse me. I didn't realize you two were having your own private party in here." She giggled.

That was it for me. "We're not!" I shouted. I turned away from Lenny and stomped out back to the party. I went right up to Tony and asked him if he wanted to dance. Lenny came out and danced with Renee.

That's the way it went after that. I danced every dance, but never with Lenny. And he, who always said that dancing more than one or two dances tired him out, was not too tired to dance with every girl there except me.

I was miserable. As it drew closer to midnight, I realized it didn't look as if Lenny and I were going to be welcoming in the new year together after all. We were both in the same room, but we were about as far apart as any two people could be.

Midnight arrived. The lights in Times Square flashed the new year. Lenny was dancing with Ellen, and I was dancing with Tony. Jessie yelled out, "It's New Year's! Everyone start kissing!"

I stiffened. I was with Tony, but I didn't want to kiss him. Lenny was the only one I wanted to kiss, but he was holding Ellen in his arms. How I wished I had never opened my big mouth to Lenny. He was right, it wasn't his fault I had made dumb baby-sitting arrangements on New Year's Eve.

I was ready to go over and apologize to him. But then I looked over to where he had been dancing with Ellen. He wasn't there. He and Ellen had moved to the sofa where they were locked in a long and passionate kiss.

When I saw that, it was as if something snapped in me. I was so angry I didn't know what I was doing. I wanted to show Lenny he wasn't the only one who could kiss someone else.

I started out by kissing Tony. Then I went around the room, kissing every boy there. The boys all loved it. They shouted out cries of encouragement. All the other girls had kissed the boys they were dancing with, but no one else was kissing them all.

I only looked at Lenny once while all this was happening. He was still on the sofa, his arm around Ellen, but he wasn't kissing her. Instead, he was glaring at me with an expression of anger so intense that it brought me back to my senses. I stopped all kissing and fled to the bathroom.

I gazed in the mirror and hated what I saw. I had taken extra time tonight with fixing my hair and putting on makeup so I would look pretty for Lenny. I knew nothing I could do now could make me look pretty in his eyes.

The next morning I woke up with an awful headache and a sick feeling in the pit of my stomach. It took me a moment to realize why. Then the events of last night came flooding back to my mind and made me even sicker.

What I wanted to do was pull the covers over my head and forget that New Year's Eve had even taken place. But my curiosity to find out what had happened after I left the party last night was strong enough so I did make it out of bed. I grabbed the telephone and took it into the closet, the only place where I could talk in private in my house, and dialed Fran.

What she told me confirmed my worst fears. After my departure, Lenny had spent the rest of the night with Ellen. He had danced with her constantly and had left the party with her to walk her home. If I wanted to find out more, Fran told me to meet her over at Jessie's. A bunch of kids were going there to clean up the mess from the party and finish the food that was left over.

I hung up and sat there in the darkness of the closet, thinking. Lenny and I had been so close to each other recently, so happy together. How could everything have changed so fast? Could he really like Ellen again?

I felt so awful, I didn't even want to leave the closet. But I knew that unless I faced up to my problems, they weren't going to get better or go away. Ellen would probably show up at Jessie's this morning, and if there was free food, I was sure Lenny would. I wasn't going to set them up with any situations to be alone together. I had to face Lenny sooner or later. It might as well be now.

I got dressed and headed toward Jessie's. To get there, I had to pass the end of Lenny's block. As I did so, I spotted him coming out of his building.

I froze. I was tempted to run and hide, but he had already seen me. Maybe it was better for me to meet him alone, in the street, than up at Jessie's with a crowd of kids.

I was filled with conflicting emotions as he approached. The first was anger—at what he had done last night; the second was shame—at the way I had picked to get even; the third was fear—as to what he might do now. I didn't know how to react. Should I take the offensive and yell at him for the way I carried on with Ellen? Should I be nice and apologize for what I had done? Should I say nothing and see what he would do?

I decided to wait and feel out his mood. I stood there, my heart hammering, awaiting his reaction.

"What are you so angry about?" was the first thing he said as he reached me.

This was not what I expected. Here I hadn't said a

word, but he was talking to me as if he had been attacked. "What do you mean? I haven't said anything," I protested.

"You don't have to. . . . That look on your face is enough to kill. So you might as well come out with it!"

Once he had given me the opening, I fell right into his trap. I started talking, and I couldn't stop. I sounded off about how horrible he had been to carry on with Ellen and how humiliated I had been by his actions. How I had been looking forward to New Year's and how he had ruined everything for me.

Maybe if I had been watching his face, I would have shut up sooner. But by the time I saw that telltale red flush and the veins start popping in his neck, I had already said my piece. By then there was nothing I could do but shrink back in fear as he gave it to me but good.

"I ruined *your* New Year's?" He struggled to control his rage. "Well, let me tell you something, Linda Berman . . . you're the one who fixed it this way! If you weren't such a hothead and had control of your temper, if you weren't so stubborn and spiteful and didn't have to prove something all the time, we could have had a nice evening together. But no. As soon as you find me dancing with another girl you act as if I'm cheating on you and totally flip out. Talk about embarrassment, I'll never live down the way you acted— going from boy to boy and kissing every one of them!"

His face was getting redder, and his voice was getting louder. People passing in the street were staring at us. "Shh, Lenny. Not so loud," I begged him, but he paid no attention. He was too angry now.

"How could you? How could you let all those boys get cheap kisses from you that way? Especially that no-good Tony Hall. Do you know how many people came up to me last night and asked how I could keep going with someone as wild and crazy as you? All I could tell them was I just didn't know!"

I stared at him as the meaning of what he said sank in. People were asking him how he could go with me. He didn't know. Did that mean he was going to break up with me? How could I stand it?

"W-w-what are you going to do?" I asked, my lip trembling.

His anger seemed to dissipate a little. "I told you—I don't know. I need some time to think about things, to find out how I really feel. Right now I'm going over to Jessie's to get some of the leftover food. Is that where you're going?"

"T-that's where I was heading when I ran into you. B-but I won't go if you don't want me to."

He shrugged. "You can go—that is, if you can face up to everyone."

Facing everyone was the last thing I wanted to do, but I knew if I didn't do it now, it would only get harder. "I can face anyone you can face," I said with more confidence than I felt.

We walked together toward Jessie's in silence, each engrossed in our own thoughts. I didn't know what I could say to Lenny to make the situation better. I could see now that I had behaved terribly. It was all because I was jealous and angry and couldn't control my temper. How I hated myself for being that way!

When we arrived at Jessie's, Lenny walked straight to the living room, where most of the remaining food was. I went into the kitchen and busied myself washing bowls and dishes so I didn't have to speak to anyone. Soon Fran and Donna joined me, and as I was telling them what was going on with Lenny and me, in walked Kathy, Renee, and Jessie.

I hesitated, not sure if I could trust them or not. But Ellen wasn't there, and I needed feedback from the girls. So I told them how sorry I was for acting that way at the party.

"What are you apologizing to us for, Linda?" Renee looked at me as if I were crazy. "What's the big deal about sharing some kisses, anyway? I did the same thing myself recently, when it was my birthday. All the boys wanted to give me some birthday kisses, and they got together and cornered me in your hallway. So I kissed them all. Nobody made a big deal of it. Why would they?"

"On your birthday? Kisses?" I repeated. "Was Lenny there?"

"Sure. He was the one who set up the whole thing. He grabbed me and held my arms so all the boys could get to me. Then he took his turn."

"You see, Linda. I keep telling you about Lenny," said Donna. "It's just like him to get angry at you for the same kind of thing he does himself."

"He wants everything his own way," said Fran. "He does whatever he wants to and expects you to do what he wants you to as well. He's got you right where he wants you."

I was horrified at all this. The girls were right. Lenny did have me right where he wanted me. Not that I should have acted that way last night, but he didn't have to make me feel like a criminal about it. Especially when he had done the same kind of thing with Renee. He probably thought it was fine for him because he was a boy and could do whatever he liked. Well, I'd show him that it didn't work that way!

I was about to storm into the living room and let

Lenny know exactly how I felt in front of everyone, when the doorbell rang. That gave me a chance to calm down a bit while Jessie went to answer it.

When I saw who was there I was grateful I hadn't started another scene. It was Sheldon, and with him was Tony Hall.

My stomach tightened. Tony was darkly handsome and could be a real charmer, but he still frightened me. Last night had illustrated how dangerous he could be to me. I didn't need any more trouble.

"Hi, guys. The boys are in the living room," I said and darted back into the safety of the kitchen.

The rest of the girls went back to the living room. Fran and Donna followed me into the kitchen.

"I think that Tony likes you," said Donna. "You ought to play up to him a little and make Lenny jealous. He deserves it, the way he takes you for granted."

I began to explain to Donna how I didn't want to do anything else to put stress on my relationship with Lenny. My explanation was interrupted by shouts coming from the living room. We rushed in to find Tony and Lenny, face to face and looking as if they were about to fight.

"Why do you keep coming around this neighborhood anyway, Hall?" Lenny demanded. "You don't belong here. You don't live here. Why don't you go back where you came from?"

"I can go anywhere I damn please, Lipoff. What's it to you?"

"I'll tell you what's it to me. I don't like you moving in on our girls, that's what."

Tony and Lenny moved closer and glared at one another. I shuddered, afraid they would start swinging at each other. Before they could, Sheldon stepped in between them.

"Calm down, Lenny. Tony's a good guy; take my word for it. You've got to give him a chance."

Tony seemed grateful for the interference. He took a step back and managed a smile. "Look, Lipoff. I don't have any intention of moving in on anyone's girls. I just want to hang out and play some ball and have fun."

"Well, as far as I'm concerned, you've had your warning, Hall," Billy broke in. "The next wrong move you make you're going to have to answer to me!" He smacked his fist into his palm menacingly.

"Hey man, cool it! No harm's been done, and we don't want anyone to get hurt here," Tony said. "Let's be cool and stay cool."

"As long as you keep out of my territory, Hall—if you know what I mean." Lenny had to get in the last word.

"Sure, sure." Tony put on his most charming smile.

"Good. Now why don't you guys shake on it and consider the matter settled," said Sheldon. You could see he really wanted peace between his friends.

"Shake on it? We don't have to go that far." Lenny gave a little laugh. "Just as long as we understand each other. We'll have peace—for the new year."

"For the new year," Tony repeated, still smiling.

Lenny looked away from him and noticed me standing with the other girls at the entrance to the living room. He walked over to me and sighed.

"While I'm at it, I guess I might as well make peace with everyone. What do you say, Linda?"

I thought of what I knew about him and Renee, and really was dying to say something about it. For once, however, I was able to control my big mouth. If Lenny was willing to forgive me, I would forgive him, too.

I shrugged my shoulders in a gesture of surrender. "Well, since it's New Year's." I managed a smile. "But Lenny, let's really try to have peace this time!"

He put his arm around me and hugged me in front of everyone, and I was glad that I hadn't said anything. It was far better to be happy than to be right all the time.

Chapter

Nine

THE LONG, COLD, DREARY STRETCH of winter that set in after New Year's was never my favorite time of year. This year, at least, I had something to brighten it, and that was Lenny, of course. When I was with him I hardly minded the miserable weather or the darkness. Still, the fact that we couldn't stay outside for long made things more difficult for us.

Unless we went to Lenny's house, which always made me feel guilty because my parents disapproved of it, it was hard to be alone together. If we went to my house, I would have to bribe my brothers to let us use their room and to leave us in peace. Even so, they always had a wise remark to make, an excuse to run in and disturb us. And of course there were my parents, always throwing us condemning looks.

As a result, Lenny and I had to be resourceful enough to find places to be alone. The landing of the staircase of my building between the second and third floors was one of them. We would sit on the steps, arms around each other, talking and kissing for hours at a time. If we heard the elevator or an apartment door opening, we would pull apart and try to look as if we were having a casual conversation. The moment the coast cleared, we would be back in each others' arms again.

Another place was the back booth of the candy store. Lenny would order an ice cream soda or sundae, and I would share it with him. We would eat it slowly, trying to justify the time we spent occupying the booth holding hands, talking, or gazing into one another's eyes.

Eventually, Harry, the candy store owner, would notice us and kick us out. "Hey you two, I need this booth for someone else. I can't make a living based on your love!"

Love! My heart swelled just from hearing Harry say the word. It made me feel good to think that what Lenny and I had was so strong that even strangers like Harry could see it. And the more we went through together, the stronger my feelings for Lenny seemed to grow. Then end-term report cards came out.

As soon as I came home from school and saw Lenny standing on the corner, I could tell something was wrong. Instead of the usual warm greeting and the suggestion we go to his house or sit in the hall or the back of the candy store, Lenny gave me an abrupt, "Hi!", then promptly ignored me. He situated himself in the midst of the crowd of kids, as far away from me as he could get.

The talk of the day was about report cards, and Lenny had nothing to say. It didn't take me long to realize this must be because his report card was bad news. But I never expected it to be as bad as it was.

"You failed two subjects!" I repeated in disbelief when I finally got him alone in my hallway to admit the news. "But . . . but Lenny! You were doing so well! What happened?"

"I miscalculated my cuts in those classes. When you get too many, you automatically fail." He said this with a shrug as if it didn't really matter. "No big deal. I'll make it up next term."

I was horrified by his attitude. I didn't understand how Lenny could take anything so important as failure in school so lightly. Why, if he didn't change his ways, he could ruin his entire future!

Because I was so worried about him, I once again tried to control the situation. I started checking up on him again. I questioned him daily about whether he cut, where he went, whom he saw, and what he did. I questioned other people about him, too. I had stopped trusting Lenny and therefore kept trying to catch him in a lie.

This affected our relationship negatively. We argued more, having fights that lasted longer. I knew things weren't as good as they used to be, but I wasn't aware of how bad they had gotten until the end of February. That's when I found out about Sara Denver.

It came up during one of our typical arguments. I told Lenny I had found out he had cut school early and gone to the poolroom. He got angry enough to blurt out, "You'll have to make up your mind whether you can accept me the way I am, Linda. If you can't, there are other girls who can!"

That was all I needed to hear. I was sure this remark wasn't something that just flew into Lenny's head. There was something going on I didn't know about.

Despite the fact it took me a long time to get it out of Lenny, I suspected he wanted me to know all along. There was too much pride in his voice when he informed me that there was a girl who lived near the pharmacy where he worked who had a crush on him. Her name was Sara Denver; she was in eighth grade in junior high, and she was very cute. He knew she liked him because she kept hanging around waiting for him to go out on a delivery and finding excuses to walk along with him.

I felt a pang of jealousy as he spoke. The thought of what it would be like to lose Lenny to another girl was more than I could bear. I didn't want to let him know that, however. "Well, you can have your junior-high-school baby if you want her—I don't care!" I tried to look as if I didn't.

It didn't work. Lenny saw right through me. He grinned and put his arm around me. "Calm down, fireball. You know there's no one who could take your place. Stop trying to change me, and everything will be fine. I'll tell that Sara I have a girlfriend so she can stop hanging around and bugging me."

I leaned back against him and felt better. But only partially. I made up my mind to be extra careful from now on. Careful not to get him angry by doing stuff like nagging him about school. And careful to watch for signs that anything might be developing between him and that Sara Denver!

It wasn't until two weeks later that I received my first inclination that something I was unaware of might be going on. It was Tony Hall who told me he had seen Lenny walking on the street with this girl one night. Right away I suspected the girl was Sara, but I didn't want to confront Lenny unless I was sure. I asked Tony to see what he could find out for me.

Of course Lenny would reveal nothing to Tony, but fortunately, Sheldon did. He told Tony that the "cute young thing" staring all starry-eyed at Lenny had been none other than Sara Denver, herself.

That horrible feeling of jealousy returned. It rose to my throat so fast I thought I would choke on it. If I had had Lenny there at that moment, there would have been no stopping me from attacking him. Fortunately, he was at work, and this gave me some time to cool off.

I called up Roz to try to unload my feelings. She had had a similar experience recently when she found out Jessie had been making a play for Sheldon.

"It really doesn't matter if that Sara has a crush on Lenny or not," she said. "What does matter is how he responds to her. If he really did make it clear to her you're the one he cares about, then I don't think you have to worry if she follows him around. If he's actually encouraging her, then you do."

"Well, Lenny did say he was going to tell her about me," I began.

"Come on, Linda," Roz scoffed. "What Lenny says he's going to do means nothing. I bet he never said a word about you."

"I wish I could find out."

"You can," Roz laughed. "I'll call him at home and pretend to be Sara. I'll tell him I heard he has a girlfriend and ask if it's true."

"You can't do that! Lenny's bound to recognize your voice. Besides, I don't want to take the chance his mother will find out what's going on."

"Then get some girl whose voice he doesn't recognize to call him. And make it at work so his mother will never know."

We decided the perfect girl would be Kathy Jones. She had a soft, young-sounding voice that Lenny wasn't familiar with on the phone. Kathy was nice, and I felt I could trust her. When I told her what I wanted her to do, she laughed and thought it would be a great joke on Lenny.

So the next night, after Lenny had gone to work, Roz, Kathy, and I met on my corner. Roz and I crowded around the phone booth in the back of the candy store while Kathy made the call.

"Hello? City Drugs? I need to speak to Lenny Lipoff, the delivery boy. It's very important."

Kathy looked at Roz and me when she said this, and we all cracked up. She sounded great! I was sure Lenny wouldn't recognize her voice over the phone. I just hoped he'd never spoken to Sara over the phone either, so he wouldn't be familiar with her voice that way.

"Hello, Lenny? This is Sara Denver. Sorry to call you at work, but I just heard something that bothered me. I hoped you could clear it up by answering a few questions.

"What are they? Well, someone told me you have a girlfriend you've been going steady with for a while now. Is that true?"

My heart pounded as I waited to hear what Lenny's reply would be. This was his chance to prove he really was loyal to me the way he said he was.

"Well, I'm glad to hear you say that, Lenny. I'll see you soon at the store."

Kathy hung up the phone and looked at me. She wasn't laughing now. "He said he's not going steady with anyone."

My stomach clutched with pain which immediately gave way to anger. "The dirty double-dealing rat!" I pounded my fist into my palm. "Wait until I get hold of him!"

* * *

Fortunately, by the time I saw Lenny after school the next day, I was a lot calmer. This meant I was able to keep myself from grabbing him around the neck and strangling him. Still, he could tell by my expression that something was wrong.

"Okay, let's have it. What are you angry at now?"

"Angry? I'll tell you what I'm angry at!" I looked around at all the kids hanging around my corner. Somehow, I maintained enough self-control not to want to make a scene in front of everyone. "Let's go somewhere we can talk in private."

"How about my house?" he suggested hopefully.

I knew what he had in mind with that suggestion. All he'd have to do was start softening me up with some hugs and kisses, and he figured I could never stay mad at him. Well, it wasn't going to work. This time I was going to be tough.

"No, not today," I said firmly. "Let's go sit in my hallway."

We sat on our spot between the second- and third-floor landings. But this time I sat down on the steps, making it quite clear I was here for business, not kissing. Lenny sat down next to me.

"Well? Why all the doom and gloom?"

Now that I had him here, I wasn't sure how to begin. I decided to start by playing it cool. "How's Sara?" I asked innocently.

"Sara?" I could see him squirm. "Why bring her up? I haven't even seen her recently."

"I suppose you haven't heard her on the phone, either."

"Phone? What do you mean, phone?"

That was it for trying to remain calm. I totally lost all composure. "I mean on the phone when she called you last night to ask if you were going steady and you—you answered *no!*"

"H-how do you know about that?" He looked absolutely shocked.

"I have my ways, Lenny." My voice rose an octave higher. "Suppose you tell me why you would tell her something like that."

For once Lenny seemed to be struggling to find the right words to say. Leave it to him—he found them. "Well, truthfully, I was only trying not to hurt her feelings, Linda. I'm not interested in Sara as a girl-friend or anything, but she is a sweet kid who has a cute little schoolgirl crush on me. It would have been cruel to make her feel bad on the phone. So I told her I wasn't going with anyone. I figured the next time I saw her in person, I would break it to her gently. I was just waiting for the time to be right, really I was. So now, tell me, how did you find out about the call?"

It was amazing, but all the anger I had built up against Lenny had left me as I listened to his words. What he said made sense. Lenny had such a good heart. He wouldn't want to hurt anyone who had a crush on him. He cared enough to wait to tell Sara about me in person. And here I was getting myself all worked up and crazy when he had done nothing wrong. I was now so ashamed of myself for doubting him that I told him the truth about how Kathy had made the call.

He stared at me in disbelief. "You . . . you had Kathy call me at work and pretend to be Sara? How could you do that, Linda? Don't you trust me at all? I didn't have to tell you about Sara in the first place if I didn't want you to know about her. She's nothing to me. Just a little girl."

"Not so little. Only a year younger than I am."

"And about three years younger in maturity. Or at least that's what I thought before you pulled this stunt. What's the matter with you, Linda? You know my boss doesn't like me to get calls at work. You could have gotten me in trouble for that alone. And involving Kathy that way. She's friends with Jessie, and Jessie has the biggest mouth in the neighborhood. Before you know it, everyone's going to hear about this and be laughing at both of us. How could you pull something dumb and sneaky like this?"

That was the start of it, and before I knew what was happening, Lenny had turned everything around. Instead of my being mad at him for something he had done, he was now mad at me for something I had done.

This was a pattern that seemed to be developing in many of our fights. No matter what it was that Lenny had done, he had a way of twisting it around and putting the blame on me. He was such a master at verbal manipulation that he would soon have me feeling guilty and down on myself.

Now he was doing it again. He gave me a long lecture on how it was terrible to try to trap another person, especially someone you loved. He said that if love between two people was to grow, it had to be based on mutual respect and trust. He trusted me, and I was going to have to decide whether I could trust him.

By the time he had finished, I felt like a dirty rat for being jealous and doing what I had done. "Oh, Lenny, I'm so sorry!" I blurted out.

He looked at me, and his face softened. "I know you are, baby." He put his arm around me. "But you've got to do better than that. You've got to start thinking before you act. And you've got to have some faith and trust in me. That's the only way things are going to work between us.''

I buried my head in his shoulder. Lenny seemed to make so much sense when he talked. He always said the right thing to make me understand the mistakes I was making. At that moment, I was actually grateful to him for being so patient with me.

"Oh, Lenny! I love you so much!"

"I love you, too, silly," he murmured.

I held him close and vowed never to distrust him again.

It wasn't too long after this incident that another occasion for suspicion arose. As the weekend approached, Lenny announced he couldn't see me on Saturday night. One of his married cousins had moved to a new house and had invited him to the housewarming party. There was going to be all sorts of great food, and his entire family would be there.

I wasn't very happy about not seeing him, but I couldn't complain about a legitimate family function. Lenny told me he would much rather be with me, but it was important to his mother that he go to the party.

I wanted to believe him, especially after his "love is based on trust" speech he had given me. But something inside me didn't quite let me.

On the Saturday night he was supposed to go to his cousin's, I decided to make the best of the situation by going up to Jessie's with some of the girls. For a while it was fun fixing each other's hair, listening to records, and creating our own ice cream sundaes in Jessie's kitchen. But my mind kept drifting back to Lenny, and wondering if he had really gone to his cousin's.

Eventually, I got to the point where I wasn't relaxed

enough to have fun anymore. I had to prove to myself that Lenny really was where he said he was.

I said good-bye to the girls, left Jessie's, and started walking up the block. When I got to the corner of Lenny's street, I was drawn to his house as if by a magnet. I decided to walk by, although I didn't know what I expected to find.

When I reached the alleyway where his windows faced, I could see that the lights were on in his living room. That was strange. If Lenny had gone to his cousin's with his mother, why would the lights be on in the living room?

My sense of uneasiness was growing by the moment. I didn't know what to do. Without fully realizing what was happening, I found my feet leading me toward the poolroom. Before I knew it, I was standing there staring at the door that opened to the staircase that led up to that dark, dingy, and disgusting gathering place of the boys in the neighborhood. Somewhere in that room was a boy who knew where Lenny was right this moment.

I hesitated before opening the door. My last unpleasant experience in the poolroom was still vivid in my mind. I didn't want to risk getting into trouble again. But I had to know about Lenny. I had to know.

I opened the door and marched up the stairs. I heard his voice even before I reached the top but I had to poke my head in to be sure. There was Lenny, bent over the table, poised to make a shot. He laughed aloud as the cue ball made its connection. He was having a grand old time.

I had seen all I needed to see. Lenny had chosen the poolroom tonight rather than take me out. But what I didn't understand was why he went to all the trouble to invent a story about his cousin just to go to the poolroom. There wasn't anything happening to-night. He could have spent some time with me, left early, and still had plenty of time for the poolroom if he had wanted to.

Something was going on that I hadn't figured out as yet. And I had this sick feeling that I wasn't going to like it when I found out what it was.

I was up half the night thinking about what I was going to say to Lenny. It was time for us to have a showdown about what was going on. At this point, I had to know the truth no matter how painful it might be. I couldn't deal with not knowing any longer.

I called for Lenny late the next morning, at the time I figured he would be waking up. His mother answered the door and looked surprised to see me. Lenny was still in bed so she had me sit in the living room while he was getting dressed.

While I was there, she bombarded me with questions. She kept trying to find out bits of information about Lenny.

I was very uncomfortable. I didn't know what Lenny wanted his mother to know and what he didn't. She kept asking about school and whether he was going. I let it slip that he had cut one day last week. I tried to cover it up, but it didn't help. As soon as he came out of his room, she confronted him with what I had said.

Lenny gave me a dirty look. "Linda doesn't know what she's talking about," he said. "As usual, she's running her big mouth where she shouldn't!"

I felt awful when he said that. How could I have been so dumb as to let his mother manipulate me? Now he had a reason to be angry at me before I even nad a chance to talk to him. I had lost all my self-righteous momentum about how he had lied to me about going to his cousin's.

In a way, it probably was good that he was angry at me. I don't think he would have told me what he did without some anger behind it. And as painful as it was to hear what he had to say, it was better that he got it out in the open.

It was a warm day for late winter, a day that hinted of the coming spring. We walked to the back of the park, and as we did, he kept lecturing me on the necessity of minding my own business and keeping my mouth shut before I got into big trouble. He was right about that, but it still didn't change the major issue. It wasn't until we found a sunny bench overlooking the Hudson River that I could get in a word about what I had to say.

"Why did you lie to me about going to your cousin's last night?" I finally cut into one of his sentences.

He stared at me open-mouthed. "What do you mean, lie to you?" He attempted to buy time.

I came right out and told him I knew he was not at his cousin's, but at the poolroom. "I also know there was no reason for you to make up that whole big story just to go to the poolroom. You must have been planning on doing something else. So what was so important that you had to go to those lengths to lie to me?"

He didn't look at me, but gazed out over the river. "You really don't want to know," he said finally.

"Yes I do," I insisted. "Nothing could be so terrible that you have to lie about it. How can we make progress together unless we face the truth?"

"Okay, you asked for it." He swallowed hard. "Remember a while back when we were fighting about school and stuff?"

113

"Uh huh."

"Well, at a weak moment I asked this girl to come to the movies with me last night. That was what I was planning on doing."

I felt this lump in my throat so big I could hardly breathe. "Girl? Who was she?" I forced out the words.

"Sara. Sara Denver. Look, Linda, it didn't mean anything! She was just there at the right moment when I was feeling angry at you. I asked her and she said yes. That's all there was to it."

"But—but you weren't at the movies last night. You were at the poolroom!"

He sighed. "I know. She broke the date. And you can thank Ellen Rossi for that. She saw Sara in school, and they were talking about me. She told Sara she used to date me at one time herself, but now I was going steady with you. That night, when Sara saw me at the store, she asked me if what Ellen said was true. By that time I had calmed down enough to realize I had made a mistake and didn't want to go out with her anyway. So I told her it was true—I was going steady and shouldn't go out with her after all." He paused and looked at me for my reaction.

If my face showed anything of what my insides were feeling, it was probably dead white. "So what happened?" I asked, struggling not to cry.

"Nothing," he shrugged. "Sara wouldn't go out with me because of you, and I was glad of it. I didn't want to hurt you, but I had already told you that story about my cousin and decided I'd better stick to it. So I went to the poolroom with the boys. Nothing terrible happened—really, it didn't."

"Nothing terrible happened? You ask out another girl and lie to me on top of it! Oh, Lenny, how could you? And after that whole speech you gave me about 'love is based on trust,' too!" I was losing control now. The tears started flowing from my eyes.

He moved closer to me on the bench and held me to him. "I know, baby. I know. I'll never do anything like that again. Please believe me."

"Believe you? How can I believe you after this?" I sniffled.

"It was just something I had to do—something I had to experience," he answered. "I learned my lesson from it, Linda. We all have lessons to learn. Maybe yours is not to open your big mouth and mine is not to do dumb impulsive things to hurt you if I get angry. I'm really sorry."

I looked at him and saw that tears were shining in his eyes, too. He was sorry, he really was. I could see it in his face.

I clung to him and felt this rush of love for him. I didn't understand it, how hurting so much could actually increase my love. But it seemed to work that way—each time we made up from a fight, it got better than ever.

Maybe it was because through our difficulties, we came to understand each other more. But whatever the reason, there was nothing I could do about it. I loved Lenny so much, I could probably forgive him anything!

I just hoped there wasn't going to be a lot more I would have to forgive.

Chapter

Ten

SPRING HAD SPRUNG, and it was glorious! The days grew longer and warmer and were filled with the sounds and smells of spring. Our crowd stopped hibernating in hallways and people's houses and returned to the park wall, where we could appreciate the main event of spring—the return of the baseball season.

The boys' team, the Royals, played official games every Saturday, but even at other times there was always something going on in the park. There were impromptu baseball games that sometimes included the girls as well; there was handball or racquetball, basketball or gymnastics on the parallel bars. Spring felt like coming alive all over again.

This was the first time I had ever had a boyfriend to share the joys of the season with. Lenny loved the warm weather and the outdoors as much as I did, and he said that seeing it through my eyes made him appreciate it even more.

One day we took a walk together to Ft. Tryon Park. We sat on a wall overlooking a flower garden bursting

116

with color. It was so beautiful there, inhaling the scent of the flowers, feeling the gentle spring breezes and the warmth of the sun on our faces. I felt so peaceful and serene.

I noticed that, without thinking, Lenny was pulling on some ivy that grew on the wall.

"Oh, Lenny, be careful! If you pull off the little suckers, the ivy can't grow right. After all, it's a living thing—look at all the tiny little leaves struggling to grow. When you think about it, we don't really know if plants have feelings, too."

"Have feelings? Plants?" He turned to me and smiled. "Only you could come up with a statement like that, Linda. I like it when you're soft and tender that way. It makes me feel calmer inside myself. When wer're together like this, I can forget about stuff like my parents and school. My insides can stop churning for a little while at least."

I looked into his eyes and smiled back. It made me feel great to have Lenny think of me this way. If only I could always be the way he wanted me to be—calm, sweet, serene, easygoing, and together. It was what I wanted not only for Lenny, but for myself.

Unfortunately, I still wasn't always able to react the way I wanted to. I still had this tendency to get hurt easily; I still said and did the wrong thing at times, and I still had this terrible temper. When I lost it, trouble was bound to follow.

This particular trouble began on a gorgeous day, right before Easter vacation. School had let out early, and Lenny had told me the night before we would take a walk down the drive by the Hudson River. It was a perfect place to appreciate the beauty of nature and a perfect place to make out.

Unfortunately, events caused Lenny to change his

plans for the day. It seemed that Chris Berland had caught Tony Hall trying to steal some money from him. Chris had promptly challenged Tony to a fight, and the boys were all worked up about it.

"Chris is big and strong, but Tony is fast and used to street fighting," Lenny told me. "This is going to be some match! I can't wait to see Chris smash Tony's face in and bloody his nose!"

"Ugh! How can you even talk that way?" I grimaced. "As if it's fun to watch someone beat someone else up and see blood. I think it's disgusting!"

"You would," he answered. "You have no sense of excitement, no appreciation of the skill and finesse involved in a good fight. Well, you don't have to come with me to watch it if you don't want to."

"Don't have to come with you? What do you mean, Lenny? Didn't you promise to come somewhere with me? To walk down Riverside Drive this very afternoon?"

"Oh. I guess I forgot." Lenny's face fell, then picked up again. "But we can walk down the drive any afternoon, Linda. We have all of vacation in front of us. This fight, however, is a one-time thing. If I don't go see it now, it'll be over without me."

This got me angry. How could Lenny cast aside a promise to me so easily? I was looking forward to this afternoon with him. With New York weather you could never tell. It could be nice today and then rain the entire vacation. You had to take advantage of each nice day you got. And here he was going ahead and ruining this one—and over something stupid like a dumb old fight!

"If you don't come with me now, it's our relationship that will be over." I said this automatically, without giving thought to my words.

Lenny didn't like this at all. "Oh yeah? Are you giving me an ultimatum?"

"Call it what you want, Lenny Lipoff. You promised you'd take me down the drive, and now you're going back on your word."

Lenny made one more effort to convince me. "Look, Linda. That was before I knew about this fight. Why don't you come with me? If it's over fast we might still have time to go down the drive. If not, we'll go tomorrow. Be flexible!"

But the thought of a fight's being more important to Lenny than my feelings was absolutely infuriating to me. "There's no way that I'm going to have anything to do with that kind of violence," I said. "If you won't come down the drive with me, I'll just have to go by myself."

"Suit yourself." Lenny shrugged and walked toward the park, where the fight was scheduled to take place.

I stormed off, full of rage. How could Lenny be so thoughtless? How could he abandon me that way? I was so furious at the way I had been treated that it wasn't until I had reached the entrance to the walkway down the drive that I hesitated. I knew the drive wasn't the best place for a girl to be walking on her own. To make matters worse, I spotted a group of four tough-looking boys coming my way. I didn't want to get into a situation where I could be trapped in the wooded areas down the drive.

I breathed easier as I recognized one of the boys. He was Matty Meagan, who lived down the block from me. He was big and tough, but he never did me any harm.

"What are you doing here by yourself, Linda?" he asked.

"Nothing," was my initial reply. But I was hurting so badly that before I knew it I was telling Matty what had happened. I told him how inconsiderate Lenny was of me, and how he couldn't wait to see Chris beat up Tony.

"Oh yeah?" said Matty. "I'd hate to see Tony beaten up myself. He's hung around with us a few times, and we like him, don't we, guys?"

"Yeah, we like Tony," Matty's three friends answered.

"And your boyfriend sure doesn't seem to know how to treat you right, does he, guys?"

"No, he sure doesn't," said the boys.

I felt good about having people to sympathize with me, even if it was only Matty and his friends. I guess that's why I went along with his next suggestion.

"Why don't you take us over to where this fight is supposed to take place, and we'll see if we can talk some sense into those guys?" asked Matty.

It seemed like a good idea to me. I really didn't want to go down the drive by myself, anyhow, and if anyone could convince Chris and Tony not to fight it would be Matty and his friends. They were the toughest kids in the neighborhood.

By the time we got to the park, however, the fight already was breaking up. Tony had claimed he had found the money on the floor and didn't realize it belonged to Chris. He had given the money back, and Chris had let him off with a warning that nothing like that had better happen again.

All the boys froze when they saw me coming accompanied by Matty and his friends. I felt really important to have them with me for support.

But I hadn't figured on the type of support they had in mind. "Which one is your boyfriend?" Matty asked me as we approached the group. I pointed Lenny out. "Why don't you go speak to him about being nice to our friend, Tony, and treating Linda right?" he then said to his friend, Spats.

Spats was the biggest and toughest looking of the group. His legs were like tree trunks and his arm muscles bulged. Next to him, Lenny looked like a toothpick.

Spats lumbered over to Lenny and grabbed him by the collar of his jacket. I thought he was going to talk to Lenny, but he began shoving him around. Then, before anyone realized what was happening, Spats pulled back and punched Lenny in the jaw.

This got me so angry that I lost all fear. I ran up to Spats and began pounding on his back. "Get away from him, you big bully! Get away from him!"

Spats whirled around to face me, his face flushed with anger. "Why, you little punk! If you weren't a girl I'd knock your teeth out!" he threatened. But he let go of Lenny, and that was all that mattered.

"Lenny, Lenny. Are you all right?" I asked anxiously.

Lenny held both hands to his jaw. I could see blood trickling down between his fingers. I felt awful to see him that way.

"I'll live," he managed to say.

Matty and his friends took off and left the park. Lenny's friends gathered around him as if he was some sort of hero. To have taken a beating from Spats and survived was no small feat.

Lenny was in no mood to be worshipped. "I'm okay, I'm okay." He shook everyone off. "I'm just going home to get some ice to put on my jaw." He turned and headed toward his house.

I ran after him. "Oh, Lenny. I'm so sorry this

happened. I had no idea Spats would hurt you. Really I didn't!"

Lenny let me accompany him to his house. He allowed me to clean up the blood and make an ice compress to put on his jaw. He listened to my explanation of how I had unloaded my feelings on Matty and his friends and how they had taken it upon themselves to teach him a lesson.

Then he really gave it to me. "So this is all *your* fault," he boomed, the rest of his face now as red as his jaw. "As usual, you couldn't resist running your big mouth. And to whom? Those punk, bully tough guys who don't know how to handle anything except with their fists. When you talk to the likes of them it's just like telling them to hit me. And look what happened. I've never been in so much pain in my life!"

Lenny was furious at me now. I listened to his tirade about how I was ruled by my emotions and had no common sense and could say nothing to defend myself. How could I when Lenny had suffered so much pain because of me?

Finally, Lenny burned himself out with his yelling. He looked at me, saw the tears that were streaming down my face, and I guessed he realized I was sorry. He gave a deep sigh, and put his arm around me. Careful to avoid his bruised side, I kissed him, trying to show him how much I did love him despite what had happened. He kissed me back, and before we knew what was happening, we were making out with more passion and intensity than we ever had before.

We were so involved in one another that we completely forgot about the time. We didn't hear his mother coming home from work until her key was already in the door.

When she came in and saw us on the bed, our

clothes all disheveled, she was furious. When she saw the bruise on Lenny's face and listened to his explanation of what had happened with Spats, she was even angrier.

"This relationship is getting entirely out of hand!" she fumed. "You're too young for all this, and it's not good for either of you. I don't want you in my house when I'm not home ever again, Linda. If I find you've been here, I won't hesitate to call your mother immediately. This type of thing can lead to nothing but more trouble, and it's got to stop!"

If there was a hole somewhere I would have crawled right in it. But I had no choice but to sit there and take Mrs. Lipoff's wrath. Angry as she was, I knew my own parents would have been even tougher in the same situation.

So I tearfully apologized and promised it would never happen again. I went into the bathroom to comb my hair and straighten up my clothes. I looked at Lenny before I left and was frightened by the hardness in his eyes.

"What's going to happen to us?" I whispered.

"I don't know," he said tersely. "Why don't we wait and see."

I could tell by the sound of his voice that it didn't look good for us.

Lenny broke up with me the very next day. We were sitting on the steps of my hallway, and he told me he had had a long talk with his mother and decided she was right. We were no good for one another. To continue our relationship would bring us more trouble.

Then he asked for his ring back. In shock, I took it off my neck and handed it to him. This ring that I had become so used to wearing it was almost a part of me—he was taking it back. I couldn't believe it!

I was already in a very fragile state when this happened. I had been up most of the night thinking about the events of the day and how horribly everything had turned out. I had feared the worst with Lenny, but was in no way ready to accept it.

As I watched him put the ring in his pocket, the reality of what was happening hit me. "No, Lenny, don't do it!" I actually begged him. "I'll never do anything like that again—I learned my lesson this time. Don't go. I love you. I love you so much!"

But Lenny had made up his mind. Nothing I said had any effect on him. "It's better this way, Linda. Believe me," was all he said before he turned around and ran out of the building, leaving me there crying on the staircase.

My parents must have heard all the noise we were making in the hallway. They came out and brought me back into the apartment. By this time, I was crying hysterically.

The thought of losing Lenny after all we had gone through together, after the wonderful times we had shared, after all the deep conversations, all the love and understanding, was more than I could bear. Add to that the guilt I felt at having gotten him hit and the embarrassment of having his mother find us in her apartment, and I totally lost control.

I threw myself on the bed and cried. I cried for what we had together and lost. I cried for the future times we would never know. Lenny was the most important thing in the world to me. How could I live without him?

I cried for what seemed like hours. My parents stayed with me the entire time and tried to comfort me. This only added to my feelings of guilt because of all the times I had fought with them over Lenny.

In the midst of my hysterics, I wound up telling my parents everything. I told them about the things I had done and the times I had disobeyed them. I told them how sorry I was and how I hoped they could forgive me.

Surprisingly, my parents didn't go crazy like I thought they would. "We're glad you could finally tell us these things, Linda," my mother said softly. "The important thing is that you learn from this—that you realize this kind of involvement with that boy is detrimental to you. He's not right for you; he has too many problems. But even if he didn't, it still wouldn't be healthy for you to be so preoccupied with him."

"That boy has become the focus of your life," my father pointed out. "It's not good to put so much importance on someone else, especially at this point of your life."

"There are too many other things that should be important to you," said my mother. "School, your friends, family, activities you can do without a boy. With that boy, your life was becoming out of balance. It had to end like this, with your getting so hurt. And the last thing we want is to see you hurt."

"Well—well, it's too late for that," I sobbed. "I don't know how I can face the future without Lenny. What am I going to do without him?"

"I have faith in you, Linda. I'm sure you're going to manage." My mother patted my hand. "But you don't have to worry about your entire future right now, you know. Just get through each day the best you can, and the future will take care of itself."

"Okay," I sniffled. "But how do I get through

today? I don't think I can go out there and face everyone in the crowd in the state I'm in. I just can't.''

"You don't have to," my mother said. "This is Easter vacation. How would you like to take a real vacation and get away from the neighborhood and its problems for a while?"

"Vacation? Where, Ma?"

"You could go out to Long Island and stay with your grandmother, Aunt Ruth, and Uncle Al for a while. You can spend time with your little cousins, Joyce and Iris. That should cheer you up."

"Stay at Grandma's?" I repeated. I hadn't gone to visit my grandmother for ages. In fact, I hadn't seen anyone in my family for a long time. I felt a twinge of guilt for this neglect. I had always been especially close to my Aunt Ruth and Uncle Al, and my little cousins were adorable. They probably would cheer me up.

"Okay," I smiled through my tears. "Call up Grandma and see if you can arrange it. I want to go as soon as possible."

That very afternoon I found myself on the Long Island Railroad, heading out to Grandma's. I had talked to Roz, Fran, and Donna before I left to tell them why I wouldn't be around during Easter. They had all been sympathetic, even Donna, who only rubbed it in once about how she had always told me Lenny was no good for me.

The farther away I got from Washington Heights, the better I felt. The pain was still there, but I didn't have to concentrate on it. I could concentrate on how nice it would be to have this time to spend with my family.

When I was little, I used to go to Grandma's a great

deal. Since I was her first grandchild, I was special to her. Aunt Ruth and Uncle Al didn't have any children then, so I was special to them, too. When my cousin Joyce came along, she came to look at me almost as a big sister, but I never fought with her the way I did with my brothers. Cousin Iris was still a baby and really adorable. I did love to go to Grandma's, where everyone made me feel good all the time.

Uncle Al picked me up at the station and lifted me high into the air as if I was still a little girl. "Hello, stranger. Good to see you," he laughed.

"Linda's here! Linda's here!" Blond, blue-eyed Joyce came flying out of the house when she saw I had arrived. Aunt Ruth and Grandma gave me hugs, and baby Iris clapped her hands joyfully. She had gotten so big since I had seen her last, I could hardly believe it.

The house was filled with the wonderful smell of baking. "Cookies. I made them in your honor." Grandma smiled.

I hugged her in appreciation. Sometimes it amazed me what my grandmother could do. Her hands and feet were so crippled by arthritis that it was hard for her to walk or pick up things. Even so, she managed to do things like knit sweaters and bake cookies and take care of little Iris, and it was all done with love.

There was so much love for me in my grandmother's house that I felt tears come to my eyes. I didn't deserve it. There were many times I could have come to see my family over the last nine months, but I chose to be with Lenny instead. No one seemed to hold it against me. It was great to be loved so unconditionally.

That loving feeling got me through the week. Aunt Ruth and Uncle Al planned all sorts of activities for Joyce and me. One day we went bowling, another day to a little amusement park, still another to the movies. We barbecued in the back yard, something I never got to do in the city.

Grandma told me stories of what it was like for her as a little girl living in Europe. She had had a very hard life. Her mother had died when she wasn't much older than Joyce. She had lived through illness, poverty, and war. She had been left a widow when her children were still young. And her arthritis brought her pain every day.

Listening to her made me put my problems into perspective. As painful as my breakup with Lenny was for me, I still had it pretty good. I had parents who cared for me, friends I liked, good health, and the opportunity to grow up and be whatever I decided to be.

Grandma made me understand my parents a lot better, too. She told me how my father worked so hard at a job he didn't like so our family could have what we needed. She pointed out how my mother always put her children first, too.

"I know you think your parents are too strict and too demanding sometimes, Linda. But you have to remember they've been around longer than you have. They've learned from experiences similar to what you're going through and would like to keep you from making mistakes and getting hurt. All parents want that for their children."

She sighed when she said that, and I wondered if she was thinking of mistakes she had made in her life.

"I understand, Grandma," I said. "But parents can't always keep their children from making mistakes. Sometimes people only learn from going through a bad experience."

"That's true." She reached out and brushed away

the hair that was falling in my eyes with her crippled hand. "And I hope that while you're here you'll do a lot of thinking about what you can learn from your experiences."

That's exactly what I did do. Joyce was ten and a half, an age where she was first starting to have some interest in boys, and every night she asked me to tell her about what it was like going with Lenny. I told her stories starting way back when we were first going together. I told her about all the ups and downs, the good times, and the fights and breakups. I told her how bad I felt because I thought this time it was going to be for good.

I don't know how much Joyce understood, but it was good for me to talk about it. It helped me to look at the whole picture of my relationship with Lenny. It helped me to see how obsessed I had become with him. I had wanted to fix him, change him, make him better, keep him from making what I saw as mistakes in his life.

I saw now that I couldn't do it. If parents couldn't make everything better for their own children, how could I possibly expect to do it for Lenny?

I had to let go of him and start going on with my own life.

Chapter

Eleven

As long as I was away in Long Island, it was easy for me to be strong about my vows to let go of Lenny. Once I returned home, I knew it was going to be much more difficult.

I came back to Washington Heights on a Sunday. I dressed especially nicely for the trip, wearing a skirt with a matching top. I purposely kept my good outfit on when I went to meet Roz and Fran by the park. No one was there, so we decided to walk to the school-yard. My friends filled me in on what had gone on while I was away.

Both Sheldon and Danny had apparently been influenced by the fact that Lenny had broken up with me. They had come to Roz and Fran and told them it would probably be a good idea to cool things off in their relationships, too. They had decided they would date each other when they felt like it, but they would also date others. As for Billy and Donna—they had been fighting a lot over vacation, and it looked as if they might break up completely or come to an agreement to date others as well.

"Wow!" I commented as we approached the schoolyard. From a distance, we could see the boys did have a game going on. "So everyone's relationship is messed up."

"I don't consider it messed up." Fran took off her thick glasses and shoved them in her purse. That was a sure sign she was preparing to flirt with someone. "I've been wanting this agreement with Danny for some time now. He's going away to college next year, and how often will I get to see him? Besides, to tell you the truth, there's this boy in Bio class I went out with one time. I felt guilty about it and didn't go out with him again. Now I can go out without feeling like I'm cheating on Dan. I don't have to feel tied down. And if Danny and I work out in the long run, none of this will matter. I think it's better this way."

"Do you feel that way, too, Roz?" I asked.

"Basically, yes," she answered. "There are some cute boys at school I'm interested in going out with—although I can't say I feel good about the thought of Sheldon's going out with other girls."

"The thought of Lenny's going out with other girls makes me feel sick to my stomach," I admitted. "But there's nothing I can do about it now that he doesn't want me anymore."

Even though Lenny didn't want me anymore, you could tell he was reacting to my appearance at the schoolyard. He missed an easy catch and kept looking over to where we girls had sat down on the steps. I saw all this out of the corner of my eye because I refused to look at him directly.

When the inning was over he came up to where we were sitting. My heart beat faster as he approached.

131

He looked so adorable, his face glistening with sweat, his hair all messed up from playing ball. Part of me wanted to keep looking at him and drink in every detail. Part of me didn't want to look at him at all.

He spoke to me first. "Hey, Linda. I'm missing my favorite baseball glove. Could I have left it at your house?"

I stared at him coldly. "Could be."

"Well, can you get it for me?"

"If you want it, Lenny, you're going to have to come up and get it yourself—preferably when I'm not at home, too."

"Okay, okay. If you want to be that way." He shook his head and walked over to talk to some of the boys.

I said very little to him for the rest of the afternoon. I made sure he could see me laughing and flirting with the other boys, especially Louie, who hadn't been going with anyone since he broke up with Renee, and Nicky, who had always had a soft spot for me.

Outwardly, I appeared to be having a great time, but inwardly, I kept trying to swallow this lump that was stuck in my throat. I knew that no matter how I pretended otherwise, Lenny was the only one I cared about. It was going to take a lot of hard work on my part to get over him.

I started by working on school. School was the place where Roz and Fran had met other boys. It was the logical place for me to look for someone. Of course I had gone through almost the entire school year not paying attention to anyone because no one could compare to Lenny.

But now I started to take a second look at the boys in my classes. Although I was officially in ninth grade, I was advanced in some of my classes and took them with tenth graders. Tenth-grade boys were at least a little more mature.

Math was one of my tenth-grade classes. Since it was right before lunch, I often wound up eating with kids from that class. One of those kids was a boy named Sandy.

Sandy wasn't bad-looking when he took off his glasses. He had nice blue eyes and a serious smile. He was very bright, and we often discussed math problems together. He was always well-mannered, and went out of his way to be nice to me. I figured he liked me but would never try anything because he knew I had a boyfriend.

I liked Sandy, but it wasn't until I broke up with Lenny that I gave any thought to his being boyfriend material.

"What did you do over vacation?" Sandy started a conversation with me on Monday as soon as he brought his lunch tray to the table.

"I broke up with my boyfriend," I answered matter-of-factly.

Sandy's eyes grew wide, and I knew he was interested. He wasn't the type to rush into anything like asking me for a date. But he did mention that I ought to come to the after-school dances held at Tech each month. "The one for May is coming up next Thursday. It would be fun if you would come."

"I'm glad you told me that, Sandy," I said with a smile. "I'll certainly try to come now that I know you'll be there."

I could tell by the relieved look on Sandy's face that it was probably a big effort for him to have even asked me to come to the dance. I knew from our previous conversations he had never had a girlfriend. I bet he had never even gone out on an official date.

I knew that Sandy could never replace Lenny in my heart. But at least it felt good to know that someone was interested in me. And just the act of going to the Tech dance made me feel better about myself, because a lot of boys asked me to dance.

I think maybe the fact that I had once been a tomboy and therefore felt comfortable talking and joking with boys helped. I noticed that most of the girls stood around in groups by themselves and never got asked to dance. I could see why, too. If I were a boy, I would never approach a whole group of girls and pick out one to ask to dance. If she said no in front of her friends, it would be too embarrassing.

So I made sure to keep away from groups of girls. I talked to the boys I knew and smiled at the ones I thought I might like to get to know in a friendly way. The results were that I got asked to dance more than some girls who were lots prettier than I.

Sandy asked me to dance several times. He was a decent dancer and a good height for me. Lenny, who must have grown four or five inches since I had started going with him, was now too tall to be really comfortable. But of course there was no electricity with Sandy like there was when I was in Lenny's arms.

When I realized what I was thinking, I put the thought out of my mind. It did me no good to compare other boys with Lenny. We had been going together a long time. I had to force myself to keep doing the kinds of things I was doing now to try to get him out of my heart.

The next big thing I did in my attempt to purge myself of Lenny was to accept a date to the movies with Danny. At first, I was reluctant to do this. "What about Fran?" I asked.

"Come on, Linda. You know Fran and I have this agreement we can each date other people. So far she's the only one to have taken advantage of it. It's time I went out with someone else, and there's no one I'd rather go out with than you. How about it?"

I wasn't sure what to say. I liked Danny, but only as a friend. I thought it would be good for me to go out with him, but I didn't want him to get the wrong idea and think I might have romantic interests in him. That would create problems I didn't need. "I'll go— as long as you understand this is a friendly date and nothing more," I told him.

"Of course I understand." He grinned.

Despite this understanding, Danny put his arm around me as soon as we walked out of my building on Saturday night. I was about to protest this action when I spotted Lenny. I immediately made the decision to let Danny's arm stay where it was.

Lenny was sitting on a car across the street by Billy's house. With him was Joel Fudd, a boy from the neighborhood Lenny had been spending a lot of time with since he had broken up with me.

Joel was very good-looking. He had curly brown hair and an angelic face. He also had a fresh, insulting mouth that rivaled Lenny's. That didn't stop the girls from flocking around Joel. He had a reputation for leaving broken hearts wherever he went.

It was just like Lenny to become friendly with Joel after our breakup. He probably figured he would benefit from any excess girls that Joel cast aside.

Tonight, however, there weren't any girls with Joel and Lenny. The two of them sat there as if waiting for Billy. But instead of watching the entrance to Billy's building, it was clear they were watching Danny and me.

135

We crossed the street to go to the theater. Lenny waved at us and grinned this maddening wide-mouthed grin.

"You two be sure to have a good time in the movies now," he called out. You could tell by the way he said it that a good time was the last thing he wanted us to have.

"Don't you worry about that, Lipoff," Danny called back. "We definitely will." He tightened his arm around me, and I was grateful for the physical contact. I was feeling sick enough then to need all the support I could get.

Unfortunately, Danny felt like continuing this type of support far longer than I felt like receiving it. Once we were in the movies and he had his arm around me, he wanted to keep it there. I didn't want him to, but I didn't have the heart to tell him. How could I when he was taking me out and being so nice to me?

I did, however, make sure he wasn't going to kiss me. "Remember, this is a 'just friends' date," I said when I found his face getting too close to mine. He backed off, only to try again a few minutes later.

"Come on, Danny, didn't we have an agreement we'd go out only on a friendly basis?" I had to say again.

"We did. So what's wrong with a friendly kiss?"

"I learned a lesson about friendly kisses on New Year's," I said bitterly. "I no longer believe in them."

"Too bad, because I do." Danny laughed. "But maybe you'll change your mind and we can have some real kisses someday."

"Maybe someday. If I ever get Lenny out of my system."

"You'd better. I never could figure out what you saw in him to begin with. If you're still stuck on him after all the crap he's done to you, all I can say is you're hopeless."

"I know," I admitted. And I was more hopeless than Danny ever knew. As he walked me home later that night, I kept looking around in the hope that Lenny might show up again.

He didn't disappoint me. When we got to my corner, we saw Lenny, Joel, and Billy hanging out in front of the candy store as if it was their favorite place to spend a Saturday night. They blocked the way as Danny and I were about to enter.

"Trying to go somewhere you're not wanted, Kopler?" Billy challenged in his tough-guy way.

"You've got that wrong, Upton." Danny was not one to scare easily. "I'm going somewhere I *am* wanted. I want a soda and Linda does, too."

"Well, go get the soda by yourself, Kopler," Lenny said. "I have something I want to say to Linda. After I'm done talking to her, she can come back here and join you."

"She's not going anywhere," Danny growled. "She's my date, and she's staying with me." He clenched his fists.

I was afraid that Danny was crazy enough to attempt to fight the three of them. Lenny and Joel weren't fighters, but Billy was, and he fought dirty as well. He'd kill Danny in no time. It was something I didn't want to see.

"Hey, come on. There's no reason to fight. I'll go listen to what Lenny has to say, Danny. Then I'll come back and have a soda with you. It's okay, really."

"Well, if you're sure it's okay." Danny went into the candy store and sat in a booth. Billy and Joel remained outside guarding the entrance. Lenny steered me into my hallway and we sat on our usual spot on the staircase.

"Linda, I've been doing some thinking," he began.

"Really? How unusual," I said sarcastically.

"Come on, Linda. This is serious. And it's hard for me to say."

My hopes picked up when I heard him say that. Anything difficult for Lenny to say probably had some connection to admitting he was wrong. "Okay, I'm listening. Go ahead."

Lenny began to talk then, in that deep, dramatic way he had I never could resist. I sat there listening to him as if I were mesmerized. I heard him say how upset he had been by being punched by Matty and then by having his mother walk in on us. He had been in a very emotional, very confused state. His mother kept lecturing him on the evils of going steady and how he was going to ruin his life tying himself down to me and not having the experience of going out with other girls. His friends had agreed. He had thought breaking up with me, painful as it was, was the best thing he could have done for both of us.

"When you think about it, there is a lot of sense to what they say," he sighed. "I mean, we're so young and all that. We won't be ready to even think about getting married for years and years, and there are lots of problems in having a long-term relationship. If we go steady all that time and never have a chance to go out with anyone else, we're bound to resent it some-day and wonder what we've missed. It's better to find out now."

"So? Have you been finding out now?" I asked painfully.

His face turned red. "Well, I've been going out with a few girls," he admitted.

"A few? Anyone I know?" I decided to torture myself by asking.

"Well, you don't really know Sara—although you heard plenty about her." The pain got worse as he mentioned her name. "I finally took her out—twice, in fact, to make sure I really felt the way I thought I did."

"And what was that?"

"That she is too young for me. Not so much in age but in maturity. She looks good and all that, but talking to her is like having a conversation with a little girl."

"Oh." This wave of relief swept over me. "And what about the others you dated?"

"Actually, there was just one other. Rachel, this girl in Fran's building."

"Oh, that Rachel." I squirmed. Rachel was a year older than I was. "You couldn't have found her to be immature."

"No. Rachel is very mature. Nice and polite—a real lady. The only problem is she's boring."

"Oh. That's too bad." I tried not to show how happy I was to hear this. "But why are you telling me all this, Lenny? Now that we're not going steady, we shouldn't even discuss people we date."

He took a deep breath. "Because dating other girls has made me start thinking. You see, I didn't have as much fun with Rachel or Sara as I would have had with you. We had some fantastic times together, Linda—that wasn't the problem with us. We ran into trouble by getting so involved that we tried to tie each other down and tell each other what to do."

"That's true," I admitted. "But what are you trying to say?"

"That if the problem comes from getting too involved, we might be able to try it another way."

"How's that?"

"By making sure we don't get too involved again. By keeping it simple, taking it easy, keeping from developing complications. By looking at each other as if we were any other girl or boy we went out with."

"Went out with? Are you saying we should go out with one another again?" I felt my heart beating rapidly.

"Sure. Why not? We could probably handle going out once in a while, on a casual basis. Just because we're not going steady anymore shouldn't mean we have to totally keep away and deprive ourselves of one another's company. After all, we still like one another's company, don't we?"

He looked at me hopefully when he said that. He looked so adorable that any antagonism I was feeling totally disappeared.

"I guess," I admitted with a reluctant smile.

"Great! Then it's settled!" He jumped up from the steps, pulled me to standing, and wrapped his arms around me. "Our new relationship—Linda and Lenny, light and easy. Enjoying one another and others, too. No ties, no complications."

"Light and easy. No ties and no complications." I laughed as he kissed me lightly on the lips. At that moment, I actually believed this was something that might work for us.

Chapter

Twelve

MY PARENTS were not happy to hear about my new relationship with Lenny, not even after I explained we were still going to go out with others and take it "light and easy."

"Once you're seeing that boy, that's it," my father said angrily. "You'll drift right into your old behavior patterns again."

"You're wrong, Daddy. You'll see." I made up my mind to make every effort to remain as independent from Lenny as I could. It wasn't easy.

I continued to do the things I had begun to do when Lenny first broke up with me. I flirted with Sandy and some of the boys at Tech; I went to the after-school dances and functions; I spent time doing stuff like shopping and studying with Roz, Fran, Donna and the other girls. Those were all things over which I had control. But I still had trouble controlling how I felt about Lenny.

Whenever I was with him, I still wanted him and him only. I had to fight to remind myself that he didn't belong to me, and that if I knew what was good for me I would build as much of a life away from Lenny as I could.

The first time we went out together, he took me to the Bronx Zoo. It was one of those perfect days in early June when the hot sun hinted of the coming summer. The zoo was a romantic place, filled with laughing children and their parents and young couples, walking together enjoying the animals and being in love.

I felt a part of it as I walked next to Lenny. He took my hand, and my heart swelled with the joy and beauty of the moment.

"Let's go see the tigers; they're my favorites," he suggested.

We must have spent half an hour in front of that cage. The tiger stretched, yawned, paced, and appeared to grin at us. It all seemed so special because I was there with Lenny.

It wasn't that way when I was with anyone else. My relationship with Sandy was developing. He had come to my house to study a few times and asked me to the last school dance. He was a good dancer, attentive, and sweet as could be. But I felt nothing when I was with Sandy. Compared to being with Lenny, the time I spent with anyone else was like a faded, empty dream.

I knew from speaking to my friends it wasn't the same with them. Roz and Fran were both dating boys they found exciting. Even Donna was attracted to someone else. It made me feel as if I was drifting apart from them. My friends couldn't really understand my way of thinking.

"I don't see how you can be stuck on someone the way you are on Lenny," Fran said to me. "As much as I care for Danny, there are too many boys out there for me to want to tie myself down to him. I tried it and it didn't work. It's much more fun to play the field.''

I knew that what Fran was saying was probably the way I should feel, but the fact remained it wasn't the way I did feel. Once I started seeing Lenny, I didn't really care about seeing anyone else. So when my Aunt Mildred, who was very big on cultural events, gave me tickets to an Off-Broadway show for my fifteenth birthday, it wasn't hard for me to decide whom to take.

"Why don't you ask one of your girlfriends?" my mother suggested. "Or that nice Sandy? Or Danny, to pay him back for how wonderful he's been to you?"

"I'll think about it, Ma," I answered. But there really wasn't much to think about. It was my birthday, and there was only one person I really wanted to spend it with. I asked Lenny to come with me.

The play was wonderful—a romantic one with the hero and heroine overcoming all sorts of obstacles until they finally got together in the end.

I couldn't help comparing the situation to mine with Lenny. Here it was almost a full year since we had started going together. We had already had as many ups and downs as the people in the story, and we had so many years in front of us before we could realistically hope that things might work out for us.

I was fifteen. I certainly couldn't even think of getting married until age eighteen at least. And if I wanted to finish college first, that meant waiting until twenty-one or twenty-two.

And what about Lenny? Would he ever pull himself together and have the discipline to get through school? What would he do if he didn't?

It seemed insurmountable to think of it all. It was probably better for us to do as Lenny wanted and keep our relationship light and see other people.

But deep inside me I knew that really wasn't what I wanted. No one else could make me feel the way I did when I was with Lenny. Like now, when we were so close to one another watching the play.

I felt so grown up sitting there next to him in the theater. I wore a new blue dress my parents had bought for my birthday. He wore his new shirt and a tie. He looked so handsome that I kept looking at him to make sure he was really there.

He caught me looking at him and smiled as if he knew what I was thinking. He reached over and took my hand.

We left the theater like that—hand in hand, the way I loved the most. I felt so close to him, so warm, so wonderful.

It was right to have chosen Lenny to spend my birthday with. My hopes were high.

My parents sensed I was becoming vulnerable to Lenny again. They decided to do something about it. They had been discussing what would be the best thing to do for the summer. Now they'd gone and rented a cottage in the Catskills.

"It'll be a positive experience for the entire family," my mother said when she broke the news to me. "Since I'm off for the summer, I'll be able to enjoy the country the whole time. Daddy will come up for his vacation and for long weekends. Ira and Joey can go to day camp. And best of all, Linda, you've been offered a job in the day camp as a counselor in training."

"But, Ma," I objected, "I want to be in the city

with my friends. I don't want to be stuck in the country all summer."

"It'll be good for you," she said firmly. "You'll get good experience working as a counselor, and make money, too. And you'll be away from the influences of this environment."

I knew perfectly well Lenny was the influence she was referring to, but I didn't say anything. My parents had already paid the first installment on the cottage and weren't going to change their minds.

Lenny didn't take the news of my going away well at all. In fact, he acted as if the whole thing were my fault. "If you don't want to see me all summer, that's okay, too," he said bitterly. "There are plenty of other girls around here to go out with."

At his words, I felt this sick sensation that warned me I was in danger of losing it again. I didn't want to fight with Lenny. I wanted to leave the city on good terms with him. I wanted to know that he wanted me and would be waiting for me when I came back in the fall. I wanted that so badly!

The next time I saw Lenny was on the last day of school. It was the day report cards were given out, and that was always a tough time for Lenny.

"If you know what's good for you, pretend report cards don't exist," Donna warned me. A group of us were sitting on the park wall after school had let out. "I made the mistake of asking Billy how he did, and he blew up like a crazy man."

I didn't have to ask Lenny how he did on his report card. As soon as he approached the wall I could tell it wasn't good by the way he was acting—snappy, irritable, and nasty.

It was pretty hard to keep conversation away from

grades on the last day of school, but I purposely avoided mentioning anything about my own. I knew it wouldn't make Lenny feel better to hear I had managed an average above 92.

Somehow Fran, whom I had told what my grades were, couldn't keep from sharing this information. "Looks like Linda's got the highest average in the neighborhood," she announced. "Ninety-two point six, to be exact."

"Really! That's unbelievable!" Kathy gasped.

"We'll just have to think of Linda as 'the brain' from now on," said Renee.

I saw the look on Lenny's face while all this fuss was being made. There was a moment of vulnerability, of hurt and pain. Then he took on his wise-guy, know-it-all expression.

"It couldn't be the highest average," I protested in an attempt to take the focus off of me. "I'm sure Danny or Louie did as well, if not better."

"Not me," Louie grinned. "I kind of took it easy this term since my grades had already been sent to the colleges. I only had a flat 92 average."

"Oh listen to them. Ninety-two, ninety-two point six; what in the world's the difference?" Ellen said. "Brains like you two might as well be from another planet. Don't you think so, Lenny?" She smiled sweetly at him.

"Yeah, I think so," he growled. "And they're awfully hard to be around. I've had enough of school and of people who spend all their time studying. How about getting out of here, Ellen? Want to walk me to get something to eat?"

"Sure, Lenny!" Ellen practically glowed as she jumped off the wall and walked down the block with him.

"I do not spend all my time studying!" I yelled after them. But Lenny didn't even turn around. There was no excuse I could make because excuses weren't called for here. The fact was that I did well in school and he didn't. I certainly wasn't going to do worse for him, and he didn't seem to want to do better for me. No matter how many good times we had together, when it came to school, we were worlds apart.

Lenny's bad mood about school seemed to be affecting everything. When I finally found out what his grades were, I understood why. He had so many cuts this term he had failed every subject.

It made me sick to think about it. How could anyone as smart as Lenny cut so much when he knew it meant failure? He had wasted one of the most important years of his life. No college would want him now. How could he live with himself?

I couldn't even talk to him about it. After report cards he had been showing too much hostility toward me and giving me a hard time about everything.

One of the things we fought about was the fact I had accepted a date with Danny for Friday night. "This is the last weekend we'll have together before you go away for the summer," Lenny pointed out. "I don't want you to spend it with Danny. Tell him you changed your mind."

"I can't do that, Lenny. Danny's got feelings, too. Besides, I won't be seeing him all summer, either. And next year he'll be at college, and I'll hardly get to see him at all. I want to have this chance to say good-bye to him."

Lenny's dejected expression made me feel bad. I reached out and touched his hand. "Look, I'm sorry about Friday. But there's always Saturday. We can go together to the dance at the Y.''

"That's what you think." He pulled away from me angrily. "That dance isn't for couples, it's for meeting people. Joel Fudd is bringing a bunch of girls from where he hangs out sometimes at 187th Street. It's not the kind of dance for us to go to together."

Now I was the one to be angry. "So it's not the kind of dance for us to go to together? What's the matter, Lenny? Do you think I might cramp your style when it comes to picking up some of Joel's girls? You have some nerve! Well, I have news for you. I'm going to that dance whether you take me or not. I'm going out with Danny on Friday night, too. And there's nothing you can say to make me change my mind. Nothing!"

Lenny's face got all red as he struggled not to lose his temper. "You might be right, Linda; there's nothing I can do to stop you, but I'm promising you this. If you go out with Danny Friday and show up at the dance on Saturday, that's it for us. It proves to me that you don't have any consideration for my feelings at all!"

"For your feelings? Have you ever stopped to consider that I have feelings, too, Lenny? Wait—I'll answer that. It's obvious that you don't. Because if you did, you wouldn't ask me to break a date with Danny so I could see you on Friday and in the very next sentence say you can't go to the dance with me on Saturday because it might interfere with your conquest of Joel's girls. That's too much for even me to take!" Angrily, I sprang up from my seat on the steps.

He stood up too and glared at me. "Is it? Well, that's too-oo bad, Linda. I can see that we're worlds apart on everything. And maybe that's the way it should be for us . . . apart!"

He stormed down the steps and I heard the outside door slam behind him. Oooh! He made me so mad I could scream!

I didn't back down. I kept my date with Danny on Friday. We went to the movies again, but this time there was no sign of Lenny.

This time I kissed Danny good night. It was a quick, friendly kiss, even though I knew Danny wanted more. I wouldn't be seeing Danny much anymore, and it was sad. Danny had played a big part in my life. He was like a big brother to me and always looked out for me.

"Let me give you some good advice before I go, Linda," he said. "Use this time away from Lenny this summer to get him out of your system. You'll avoid a lot of pain in the long run."

"You're probably right, Danny." I smiled at him. "But that's easier said than done. When I'm with Lenny, it's like I'm drawn to him by a powerful force beyond my control. It's so strong I can't fight it."

"That's nonsense. There is no such force. It's all in your mind about Lenny, Linda. It's all in your mind and it's up to you to control it."

It's up to me to control it. I kept repeating Danny's words in my head as I walked to the Y dance in the company of Roz and Donna. Sheldon and Billy had followed Lenny's lead and refused to take them to the dance as well. Fran had decided to skip the dance in favor of a date with some boy from school.

She was the smartest one of us, I couldn't help thinking as the dance got started. For it wasn't anything like I had hoped it would be. It took place in a huge gymnasium and was packed with kids, most of whom I didn't even know.

149

"Where did all these kids come from, anyhow?" I asked Roz. "I thought this was supposed to be a neighborhood dance."

"Riverdale," Roz answered, making a face. "Can't you tell from the fancy clothes and the tons of jewelry? Riverdale kids consider this their neighborhood Y, too."

Truthfully, I didn't feel very comfortable around all those Riverdale people. Even the boys were slickly dressed and looked as if they were in love with themselves. Fortunately, a group of kids we knew from the park wall showed up, and we gravitated over to them. Once someone asked me to dance, I felt a lot better. But the dance still had to be classified as boring.

"It looks as if none of our boys are going to show up after all," Roz commented as the night wore on without any sign of them.

"No, and that's good," I said. "We don't need them to find out the dance we made such a fuss over is nothing but a dud."

"I'm ready to go home soon." Donna stifled a yawn. "What about you two?"

"You're not going to go home without dancing with me, are you, Linda?"

I looked and saw Tony Hall smiling at me. He must have recently arrived, for I hadn't seen him earlier. I hesitated before replying. Tony still made me nervous.

"Come on," he urged. "Lenny's nowhere around. He went to some party with Joel."

"He did?" My eyes opened wide. "Where?"

"Dance with me, and I'll tell you all about it."

So I did. While Roz and Donna waited by the door, I danced a slow dance with Tony. "Okay, Tony. What's the story with Lenny?" I demanded.

"Just as I told you. Joel has this whole following of

150

female admirers who hang out at 187th Street. One of them, Lauren, threw a party tonight. She invited Joel and asked him to bring some boys. Joel took Lenny, Sheldon, and Billy with him.''

"Oh." I felt this horrible clutching sensation grab my stomach at the thought of Lenny's going to a party with the 187th-Street girls. I knew who Lauren was, but I wasn't worried about her. Everyone knew she was too madly in love with Joel to look at another boy. But Lauren had friends who were pretty and open to any boy who paid them attention. No, I wasn't happy to learn that Lenny was partying with the 187th-Street girls at all.

"Don't look so disappointed, Linda," said Tony. "You're better off having nothing to do with Lenny. Forget him. Relax. Enjoy the dance."

He held me closer when he said that. I sighed and buried my head in his shoulder in an attempt to block out all thoughts of Lenny.

"Isn't that cute? She's trying to hide her face," I heard someone comment.

I looked up and saw it was Lenny. He must have just arrived at the dance, and he was accompanied by Joel, Billy, and Sheldon. Billy and Sheldon didn't look too happy to find Donna and Roz there, but neither of them was as furious as Lenny. The worst thing that could have happened was for him to find me dancing with Tony!

I pulled away from Tony. I tried to explain to Lenny that I had every right to dance with Tony. That I was only dancing with him because he had wanted to tell me something important. But of course I couldn't tell Lenny what that something was.

I don't think anything I could have said would have

made any difference anyhow. Lenny was too angry. He pulled me aside and really gave it to me.

"If there was ever a chance for us, this killed it," he hissed angrily. "You never know when you have it good, Linda. You've always got to do something to prove you can have it your way.

"Well, now you can have it your way totally. I found out tonight there are plenty of nice girls in this neighborhood I didn't know about. I intend to get to know them all a lot better over the summer. So it's just as well we're ending it this way."

He turned his back on me then and went over to ask some girl to dance. I recognized her as one of the girls from the party he had gone to. She smiled up at him as if she really liked him, and he held her closely while they danced.

I felt absolutely sick to my stomach. How I wished I had never come to this dance. I still had a week in the city before I left for the country. How was I going to get through it knowing that Lenny was now involved with a whole new batch of girls?

Theoretically, that week in the city should have been one of the best ever. School was over; almost all the kids in the neighborhood were around before leaving for the country or starting summer jobs or summer school; all these great trips were scheduled. I should have been feeling wonderful.

I wasn't. Oh, I made the effort, all right. I joined in with the group going to the beach and with the one going to the pool in New Jersey. I went shopping with Roz and Fran; I played tennis with Donna. At night, I went to the park wall to talk and joke with the growing number of kids from different crowds that came to the park to meet and hang out. But no matter what I did, there was always this emptiness inside me. No matter whom I was with, I couldn't help wishing I was with Lenny.

I hardly saw Lenny. He kept away from the park, and rumors had it he was hanging around 187th Street now with Joel, his friends, and their girls. The few times I did spot him from a distance, he was always with someone from that crowd, so I was sure the rumors were true. This made me feel even worse.

My mother noticed how miserable I was. On Friday morning, as I was standing by my dresser packing for the next day's departure to the country and thinking of Lenny as usual, she came over and sat down in a chair next to me.

"It bothers me to see how unhappy you are, Linda," she said. "Especially when I know it's all because of that boy. You're going away for the summer now. You have the opportunity to meet some nice boys who won't treat you the way he does. Forget about him."

"Forget about him! Believe me, Ma, I'm trying. But it's hard to do . . . it's so hard!" I felt tears welling in my eyes.

My mother shook her head. "I don't understand it. A bright girl like you, Linda. You have your whole future ahead of you. There are so many boys who would be happy to go out with you. I don't understand what you want with that boy and all his problems."

"I guess it is hard to understand," I admitted. "Even for me. My mind knows all about Lenny's faults, but my heart doesn't seem to care about them. No matter what he does, my heart seems to belong only to him." I sighed. "But there are some good reasons for that, Ma, things that attract me to him that you don't see."

"Well, why don't you tell me about them? Maybe I can begin to see."

I hesitated. Both my parents had been against Lenny from the beginning. They had never really given him a chance. And of course they were upset every time they saw me unhappy because of him, which had been pretty often the past few months. I didn't really think it was possible to make my mother understand. But she was my mother, and she did care about me. Even when I fought with her I was aware of that. I decided I would give it a try.

I took a deep breath. "I'm not sure if I can explain it, Ma, but there's something special about Lenny. He's got so much energy; he's so full of life. Maybe it's his mannerisms; maybe it's the way he speaks. All I know is that when he talks, I can sit there watching him, listening to him for hours. He makes so much sense, too. You know Lenny's helped me learn more about myself than anyone else could have. He can be so understanding, so funny. And he's extremely intelligent—even if he doesn't get good grades in school."

"But school grades are so important, Linda."

"I know that. But it's not too late for him to turn that around. He can still make something of himself; I know he can. And once he grows up more he'll calm down a lot and won't do all the crazy kinds of things he does now."

"You think so, Linda. But you never know. Some people never grow up. That boy could continue his erratic and irresponsible behavior for the rest of his life."

"Maybe. But I don't think so. Try to look at it this way, Ma. Lenny has faults, but they're faults that can be overcome. And he has good points I've never found in anyone else. When things are good between us they're so wonderful that I think I could be happy just being with him forever. Even now, after all the hurt, I think I'd take him back if he wanted me. Can you understand that, Ma?"

"A little." My mother smiled a very sad little smile. "But I still think you'd be better off if you could forget about Lenny. Find someone else who doesn't have all these complications!"

Chapter

Thirteen

I KNEW MY MOTHER was right, of course. I would be better off if I found someone without the complications. But at this point, it really didn't make any difference. Lenny didn't want me, and that was what mattered.

I decided to make the most of my last day in the city. I went to the park and started playing ping-pong with some of the kids who were there. Tony Hall came over and challenged me to a game.

Tony was a good player, and I had to concentrate on the game very hard. So hard that I didn't even notice that Lenny was coming up behind me. The first inclination I had he was there was when I heard his voice insulting me.

"Well, it looks like garbage is attracting garbage around here. It's a good thing I haven't been hanging around this park recently—it's really starting to smell."

I swung wildly and missed my shot. That made me angry, but not as angry as his words did. The nerve of

Lenny! It was bad enough he broke up with me. Why did he have to be so mean and cruel on top of it?

Furious, I whirled around to face him. "Darn you, Lenny! Who do you think you are, anyway? Tony and I are here playing ping-pong and not bothering anyone. You come along with your nasty remarks and try to stir up trouble. Well, since you're obviously too good for this park, why don't you go back up to 187th Street and hang out with your precious new girlfriends?"

He laughed at that. "You're just jealous, Linda. Jealous that while you have to hang out with low-lifes like Hall here, I've found some friends that are really worthwhile. Guys who know what's happening, like Joel, and girls who are pretty and sweet and fun to be with—not immature, temper-tantrum–throwing babies like you!"

Tears stung my eyes at the hateful, hurtful things he said to me. I felt like going over and smacking him, but I wasn't going to give him the satisfaction of seeing me lose my temper after what he had just said. Struggling to contain myself, I said, "Well, since your new friends are so wonderful, Lenny, why are you lowering yourself to be here with us? Why don't you leave us in peace and go off to wherever it is that they hang out?"

"I can't," he grinned. "Because I invited a bunch of kids over to my house this afternoon, and they're meeting me here at the park. Joel's coming and bringing his friend, Eddy, the classiest guy you'd ever dream of meeting. And of course, some of the girls . . . I think I see them coming now. Lauren! Michelle! Over here!" He waved at the two girls who were standing hesitantly at the entrance to the park.

I felt this lump in my stomach as they approached. They were cute-looking girls. Lauren was short with hair and eyes that were almost black. Michelle was taller and thinner with light brown hair and eyes. They both had an air of confidence and style that I felt lacking in myself. I couldn't help wondering what nasty things Lenny might have told them about me. I wished there was some way I could disappear from the scene without being noticed.

They did notice me, however, and looked at me with curiosity. The last thing Lenny wanted to do was to introduce me, but Tony, who knew everyone, had no such qualms. Lenny flashed him a dirty look as he told the girls who I was.

"Oh, you're Linda. We've heard so much about you!" I was surprised at the friendly way they greeted me.

"If it was from Lenny, it couldn't have been anything good." I smiled grimly.

"That's because there isn't anything good to say," Lenny retorted. "Let's get away from here and wait for Joel and Eddy by the wall, girls."

"Come on, Lenny. There's no reason why we can't all get along here." Michelle stood up for me.

"Besides, why should we wait by the wall when we could be having a game of ping-pong?" said Lauren. "How about a game of doubles?"

"Sure!" I said enthusiastically. So Lauren teamed up with me and Michelle teamed up with Tony, and we began to play. Lenny, who didn't look happy about this arrangement, went to the wall to wait for Joel and Eddy.

While he was gone, I had a chance to get to know the girls a little. Michelle liked this boy named Bobby and was frustrated because he liked someone else. Lauren liked gorgeous Joel and had to compete with the other girls who liked him. They both thought

Lenny was cute and funny, but they didn't appreciate his fresh mouth.

There was something about the girls that made them easy to talk to. Or maybe I was so frustrated with Lenny that I needed to talk to anyone who was there. At any rate, we wound up doing more talking than ping-pong playing, and Tony got disgusted and left. I ended up telling the girls about Lenny and me—how we had been going together for almost a year off and on, and how he seemed to be going out of his way to hurt me now that he had broken up with me.

The girls were sympathetic and understanding. Lauren decided she had Lenny figured out. "I bet he still likes you, but he's afraid of a serious relationship. If he really didn't care about you he wouldn't have to act so nasty."

What Lauren said made sense, and I wanted to believe her, but it was almost impossible to do so a little later when Joel and Eddy showed up. Lenny came over with them and immediately began showing off by insulting me. I was about to leave when the girls stood up for me.

"Cut it out, Lenny. We really don't want to be around you if you're treating Linda that way," said Michelle.

"What's past is past. Why don't you put aside your hard feelings and forget it?" said Lauren.

"Yeah, show you're a big enough person to forget that nonsense," said Michelle. "Why don't you invite Linda to your house with us? We could use an extra girl."

Lenny's face turned absolutely red at that suggestion. I don't think he ever would have gone along with it, except to say no would mean losing face in front of his new and important friends. He swallowed hard and managed to say, "You can come, Linda—if you really want to."

I knew he was hoping I would say no. That's why I quickly answered, "Sure, I'll come!" And I was on my way to a place I thought I'd never see again—Lenny's apartment!

I had never seen Lenny's house look so clean and neat. I bet he had spent the entire morning cleaning it for his friends, something he had never done for me.

At first I felt very uncomfortable there, but Michelle and Lauren were so nice they made it easier for me. And then I found help in an unexpected source. Lenny's "classy" friend, Eddy, seemed to be interested in me.

He asked me to dance as soon as Lenny put on a slow record. He was an excellent dancer. I closed my eyes and leaned against his shoulder. When I opened them I saw Lenny watching me, an angry expression in his face. Quickly, I closed my eyes again.

Eddy kept asking me to dance again and again. Lenny kept alternating dances with Michelle and Lauren. Finally, he came over and asked me to dance. I accepted, but purposely stood back as far from him as possible.

"I see you like my friend Eddy," he commented.

"He seems nice. A lot nicer than you've been."

"That's because he's trying to make a good impression on you. He always does that when he first makes a play for girls. Then when he gets them he drops them."

"Well, maybe that's because he hasn't met the right girl—yet," I laughed.

After that, Lenny didn't dance with me. But Joel did and Eddy did. Then Eddy asked me to come into the living room with him and watch some television. He put on the TV, but didn't really seem interested in watching it. He seemed more interested in watching me.

He put his arm around me and began telling me how happy he was to have finally met me.

Lenny came in and said the TV was too loud. He turned it down and went back to his room.

Eddy began telling me how much nicer and cuter I was than Lenny had made me out to be.

Lenny came in and said he was serving soda, and if we wanted some we could go into the kitchen and help ourselves. Eddy told him we weren't thirsty, and Lenny left the room.

Eddy told me how he had done some wild and crazy things, some of them recently together with Lenny. I told him that for some reason I was attracted to boys who were on the wild side. He must have taken that as evidence I was interested in him, because he turned my face toward his and bent down as if he were going to kiss me.

Lenny came in again. This time he announced we all had to leave since he needed to get some things ready for the party he was having at night. This was the first I had heard about a party.

"Now that we've had a chance to get to know Linda, how about inviting her to the party, too?" Eddy asked, his arm still around me.

Lenny's face got red. "I don't think that would be a very good idea," he said. "Now, let's get out of here."

I didn't let Lenny's answer get me down. I certainly didn't expect him to invite me to his party. I knew he wasn't going to let me spend any more time with Eddy if he could help it. And I wasn't really interested in Eddy, anyhow. What mattered was I had proven I could be accepted by Lenny's new friends, and even sought after by the "classy" Eddy.

Now I could leave for the country feeling I had won at least a minor victory.

That night, as I headed toward the park wall to say good-bye to all the kids, I ran into Lenny. He was on his way to the store to get the soda for his party. I was surprised when he asked me to take a walk with him.

I was even more surprised when I saw the spot we were walking to. It was the wall on Haven Avenue that overlooked the Hudson River and the George Washington Bridge. It was on this spot almost a year ago that we had admitted we liked each other. It was here our relationship had begun.

Lenny climbed up on the wall and asked me to sit next to him. When I had, he began to speak. "I wanted you to know the reason why I didn't invite you to my party, Linda. It wasn't that I was jealous about Eddy or that I didn't want to see you or anything. I just didn't think it would be a good idea for either of us."

"Oh? Why not?"

Lenny sighed and stared out at the river. "I was afraid," he admitted. "I knew if you came to the party, it would go one of two ways, both of them bad."

"What's that?" I asked.

"Well, knowing us, there would be a good chance we would wind up in a contest to show each other how many conquests we could make among the opposite sex. It would be New Year's all over again. We'd hurt each other and be angry at each other, and I wouldn't want you to go away to the country with feelings like that."

"No," I agreed. "I wouldn't either. But what's the other way you thought it could go?"

"With our getting involved with each other all over again."

"So? What's so terrible about that?" I blurted out.

He turned to me, and I was shocked to see his eyes were full of pain. "Don't you see, Linda? We were getting so serious it was scary. We're too young for the kind of relationship we were having. This is the time of our lives we should be free, having fun, getting to know other people, and getting to know ourselves. The last thing we want to do is get married in a couple of years and then regret it. I don't want to wind up in a relationship like my parents had, screaming, fighting, hating one another. If we ever do get married, I want us both to be sure it's the right thing."

I stared at him for what he had just said was overwhelming to me. I knew I had at times wondered what it would be like to be married to Lenny, but it had only been in fantasy. For him to admit that he had actually thought about marriage was something I hadn't expected. "Married? Are you really thinking about getting married?"

He blushed. "Not now, of course. But you never can tell what the future will bring. I do care for you a lot, you know."

"Well, you certainly haven't acted that way recently," I couldn't resist saying.

"I know," he said sadly. "But don't you see that I had to do it like this? The bond between us is too strong to break in a casual way. I tried, but I couldn't handle seeing you and others, too. I figured the only way to get you out of my system was to immerse myself in seeing other girls and having as much fun as possible. I had to convince myself you weren't worth seeing."

I stared at him suspiciously, determined not to let him manipulate me with his sweet talk. But he seemed completely sincere.

"So? Did you convince yourself?"

"No." He shook his head. "Truthfully, I don't think I could ever convince myself of that. But I still think I'm right. We do have to know what it's like to go out with other people. You do see that, don't you, Linda?"

I gazed into his eyes and was lost in the depth of feeling reflected there. I felt myself drawn to him by that intense magnetic pull I could never resist. I didn't understand what that special force was that connected me to Lenny. I only knew that it was there, and I was completely powerless over it.

"Yes, I see that," I breathed, still unable to pull my eyes from his.

His face came closer to mine, and before I knew what was happening he was kissing me, and I was caught up in the wonderful sensations of being in his arms. The taste of him, the touch of him, the feel of the warm summer breeze as it blew off the river. It was all I ever wanted, and I wished it would never end.

Suddenly, he pulled away from me. He jumped off the wall. "People will be coming to my house soon. I've got to go get the soda."

The spell was broken. It was back to reality. Lenny was making a party to which I wasn't invited. He was no longer mine.

As I walked up the block with him, I was overwhelmed by a feeling of sadness. How could this be happening to us when I loved him so much?

We approached the corner where we would split up—I to head for the park and Lenny for the store. I decided to get the good-byes over quickly. "Have a good summer," I began.

He put his hand on my arm to stop me. "There's something else I want to say."

"What is it?" I heard my voice crack.

"I want to know that you understand that no matter how difficult it is for us, it's better we're apart this summer. You can get to know some boys up in the country, and I'll be able to do my thing here at home. When we meet again in September, we'll both have grown. Maybe we'll be ready to start a relationship again, or maybe we'll have grown apart. But whatever happens, we'll be the better for it. Do you agree?"

A stab of pain went through me. My heart belonged to Lenny. He was the one I wanted, and I wanted him now. But I realized, painful as it was, that I was going to have to go through this summer without him. I had no choice but to accept it. Accept it now and wait and hope for the future.

"I agree," I managed to say.

"Good!" he said with a grin. "And since we're parting as friends, will you write me and let me know how you're doing?"

"Okay. That is, if you'll write me back."

"Sure I will; but you write first. So, in that case, I'll see you in September. Have a great summer, Linda."

He bent down and kissed me on my lips. Lightly this time, but it was still enough to set my heart hammering.

As I watched him walk down the block, I couldn't help wondering what life had in store for us. Would I become strong enough to keep Lenny from manipulating and sweet-talking me? Would we learn how to have a relationship without all the ups and downs? Would the intense passion we felt for one another develop into a really mature kind of love?

Only the future held the answer for Lenny and me, I realized. I took a deep breath and began walking toward my friends who were waiting for me at the park wall.

To find out what happens to Linda
in the future, be sure to read:
ALL FOR THE LOVE OF THAT BOY

ABOUT THE AUTHOR

LINDA LEWIS was graduated from City College of New York and received her master's degree in special education. *My Heart Belongs to That Boy* is her fifth novel. She has also written four other books about Linda: *2 Young 2 Go 4 Boys*, *We Hate Everything But Boys*, *Is There Life After Boys?*, and *We Love Only Older Boys*. Recently she moved from New York to Lauderdale-by-the-Sea, Florida. She is married and has two children.

Linda Lewis

Linda Lewis knows what it's like to be a teen—the ups and downs, the laughter and the tears. Read all the wonderful books about Linda Berman and her friends as they go through the fun and adventure of growing up and the discovery of first love.

First they had a club—WE HATE EVERYTHING BUT BOYS. Then they wondered—IS THERE LIFE AFTER BOYS? As always the girls are having as much fun as ever with their latest discovery—WE LOVE ONLY OLDER BOYS. But when real love strikes it's always—MY HEART BELONGS TO THAT BOY. Now the girls have been through good times and bad, laughter and tears—ALL FOR THE LOVE OF THAT BOY.

☐ WE HATE EVERYTHING BUT BOYS   68089/$2.75
☐ IS THERE LIFE AFTER BOYS?   68311/$2.75
☐ WE LOVE ONLY OLDER BOYS   69558/$2.95
☐ MY HEART BELONGS TO THAT BOY   70353/$2.95
☐ ALL FOR THE LOVE OF THAT BOY   68243/$2.95
☐ DEDICATED TO THAT BOY I LOVE   68244/$2.75

Available From Archway Paperbacks

Simon & Schuster Mail Order Dept. BAC
200 Old Tappan Rd., Old Tappan, N.J. 07675

Please send me the books I have checked above. I am enclosing $_____ (please add 75¢ to cover postage and handling for each order. N.Y.S. and N.Y.C. residents please add appropriate sales tax). Send check or money order—no cash or C.O.D.'s please. Allow up to six weeks for delivery. For purchases over $10.00 you may use VISA: card number, expiration date and customer signature must be included.

Name _____

Address _____

City _____ State/Zip _____

VISA Card No. _____ Exp. Date _____

Signature _____ 152-06